A TIME
TO REAP

A TIME TO REAP

Michael T. Hinkemeyer

A Critic's Choice paperback
from Lorevan Publishing, Inc.
New York, New York

Reprinted by arrangement with St. Martin's Press.

ISBN: 0-931773-19-9

First Critic's Choice edition: 1985

Critic's Choice Paperbacks
31 E. 28th Street
New York, New York 10016

Manufactured in the United States of America

To my parents

I would like to thank Otto Penzler for his generous gifts of time and interest.

A TIME TO REAP

1

Sarah cut rich, sweet dough into Christmas tree shapes and waited for a phone call. By a vote of 215 to 186, she'd defeated an old rival, Florence Hockapuk of Holy Spirit Parish, for the presidency of the Rosary Society. Sister Terence Cooney, ballot counter and choir director, was supposed to call regarding Sarah's investiture, which would occur before midnight Mass at the cathedral.

Emil, formerly sheriff of Stearns County, played solitaire at the kitchen table—retirement was hell—and wondered what to do for the rest of the day, and the day after that, and so on. To make matters worse, his December arthritic flare-up had arrived right on schedule, and a swollen left knee shot lances of pain up and down his leg. He was listening for the *thwack* of the St. Cloud *Morning Tribune* on the front porch, but the doorbell rang instead. Sarah wiped cookie batter from her hands, hurried across the kitchen into the hallway, opened the door and let in Emil's successor, Corky Withers, along with a blast of arctic air. The sun was huge and deceptive in a dazzled sky. Winter had arrived in Minnesota and the porch thermometer registered three degrees below zero.

"Corky!" exclaimed Sarah. "It's a couple days early, but Merry Christmas. Have a cup of coffee with us, why don't you?"

"I'd like to, Miz Whippletree," said the young sheriff, taking off his broad-brimmed trooper's hat, "but I'm in sort of a hurry. Think I could borrow a few minutes of your husband's time?"

"Come on in," growled Emil from the kitchen. "Time is one thing I've got plenty of."

Corky entered with a long-striding plowboy amble. The scent of his lemon-lime after-shave overpowered the aroma of baking cookies. He looked like a decathalon champ, lean, blond, and open-faced. His campaign slogan had been "You Can Count On Corky." Most folks thought they could. Seeing his fretful, frantic expression now, though, they might have had some doubts.

"Emil, you've got to help me," he blurted. "There've been a couple of murders.

Emil straightened in his chair. Sarah gasped.

"Who?" asked Emil. "Whereabouts?" He'd lived in Stearns County all his life. Familiar names were the last things he wanted to hear from Corky.

He didn't. "Woman by the name of Trixie Miggs," the rookie sheriff said, "and one of her two sons. Out by Tufo's Lake, near Silverton. Think you could ride on out there with me? You're the only one around here who's ever solved a murder case. We can get there in less than half an hour."

"Is Nubs Tufo okay?" asked Emil, getting up and reaching for his cane. The demon working inside his knee exchanged a pickaxe for a sledgehammer. Norbert J. "Nubs" Tufo was an old, old friend of his. They were close to being original settlers; their fathers had been.

"We can't find Nubs," said Corky dismally. "He's not in his cabin."

Uh-oh, thought Emil. Except for an old dog, Nubs lived alone now. If a killer was roaming around out there in the countryside, striking at random, Nubs would be an easy mark. "Let's hit the road," he said.

Sarah advised Emil to wear his fur cap with earflaps rather than his felt hat. He took her advice, as usual, then he and Corky climbed into the sheriff's blue-and-white Ford, left Emil's big old stucco house on the north side, cut through the downtown area, and headed south on Clearwater Road. St. Cloud, a neat, stolid, self-satisfied city of 40,000 on the banks of the Mississippi River, was all set for the holidays. It was a rare house that didn't sport at least a few strings of colored lights. Illuminated plastic figures of Santa seemed to have the lead in popularity this year, trailed closely by the Virgin Mary. Rudolph was holding his own, though, in a tight third place.

Emil sat up front in the car and savored the blasting heater. The hot air felt good on his knee. He stuck a plug of Red Man between his cheek and gum. The bracing bite of strong tobacco tasted great; Sarah didn't want him chewing in the house.

"Do you have anybody out at the crime site?"

"Poll and Gosch," said Corky, naming deputies who'd once worked for Emil.

Too bad, Emil thought.

"Bawlie Wepner's giving us a hand too," Corky said.

Emil frowned. He recalled plenty of blotters on which the name WEPNER had appeared, along with notations such as: Drunkenness, Drunkenness and Causing a Public Disturbance, Drunkenness and Assault, and Drunken Driving.

"What kind of a name is 'Bawlie,' anyway?" Corky wanted to know.

"It's Paul E." said Whippletree. "Left Stearns County once, years ago. Was going to be a baseball pitcher, and was actually damn good. He'd been signed with the old Minneapolis Millers, I doubt you'd remember them."

Corky shook his head.

"But, like a lot of kids from here, he couldn't adjust to the Outside. His record was oh and seven by the Fourth of July. So he quit and came home. It's been downhill ever since."

Corky winced, and the old sheriff knew why. Whippletree had been describing a major facet of the Stearns

County Syndrome, and Corky was no stranger to it, in spite of his apparent success.

"No need to go off to the Twin Cities and such-like to have a good life," Corky observed.

"Guess not," replied Whippletree. "I sure as hell never did."

Corky sped through the vaulting concrete underpass beneath I-94, the new superhighway that ran on into the West, but Emil paid scant attention. When he looked out over the land, he saw it not as it was now with the new roads and the shopping centers and the pastel ranch houses, but as it had been long ago. He remembered where the trails had been, and which roads were impassable during spring thaw.

"Only the tellers are," observed Corky, jerking his thumb at a big billboard on the side of the road. The billboard asserted YOU'RE NEVER DEAD AT HANNORHED and featured a cartoonish representation of what was apparently supposed to be a cat. Never Dead. Nine Lives. The artist must have taken his training at Stonehenge. Emil said nothing. The Hannorhed County Bank had foreclosed his farm after the flood of 1941.

"St. Alazara," Corky announced, as they shot through a small village.

"Almost there now," Corky asserted. "Here's St. Frederick."

Then the sheriff's car roared into Silverton, which, in comparison to the little villages, seemed a veritable metropolis. A decrepit, ivy-covered high school faced the main drag. The creamery and a grain elevator stood side by side along the Soo Line tracks. There was a grocery store, a garage, a hardware store, and a stop sign in the center of town. The Goose Step Inn ("Where Swinging Singles Mix and Mingle") stood across the street from Father Creedmore's church, the tavern flagrant with neon, the church stony and dour.

"Turn left here," Whippletree said at the stop sign.

"God, I hope nobody saw the car," worried Corky, as he pushed the accelerator to the floor and raced out of Silverton toward Tufo's lake. "I don't want wind of these murders getting out until we've got a firm handle on them."

"Right," agreed Whippletree, with little hope. Word-of-mouth in Stearns County was incredibly efficient.

"This is it," said Corky, in a choked voice, and slowed the car.

Bawlie Wepner's mail box, with his name painted on it, tilted into the roadway, and his cedar-shingled saltbox of a house squatted beneath bare, tall trees. A dirty-white Dough-Rite bakery truck stood out in front. Through the trees, Whippletree saw the dull gray ice of the lake, windswept and cleared of snow. Nubs Tufo's cabin, gray-brown and weatherbeaten, hunkered by the shore.

Just down the road from Bawlie's place, set back among the maple and poplar and spruce, was a bright yellow ranch-style house with an attached garage. Parked in front of the house was a car belonging to the Stearns County Sheriff's Department and also a black Dodge van with a small forest of antennas poking out of it.

"Oh, Jesus H. Christ," Corky Withers said. "Roy Riley's here already."

2

"Just don't start talking to the bastard," Corky pleaded, as he got out of the car and waited for Emil to get his leg unbent. "That damn Riley gets people going so naturally they don't realize until later how much they've told him. Goddamn outsider," he added, kicking at the snow.

Deputy Jamie Gosch was sitting on a couple of concrete blocks at the side of the house. He stood up, looking greatly relieved, as Corky and Emil approached. Standing next to jittery Jamie was *Morning Tribune* reporter Roy Riley, who looked as round and hard as a cannonball, and just as aggressive.

"What the hell are you doing here?" Corky asked him.

Whippletree read the situation at a glance. Courtney P. Withers, Jr. versus Roy Riley. Both about the same age, mid-thirties. Idol-handsome Corky with his country-boy innocence and his insecurities up against the savvy grit of a tough, educated Chicago kid.

"I'm on the crime beat for the *Trib*," Riley said, actually winking at Emil, whom he had never met before, "and I understand there's been a crime out here."

Riley had overheard a radio conversation, Emil realized. He didn't drive that electronically equipped van for nothing.

"So, I have to check it out. It's my job. Hope you don't mind me doing my job?" Riley smiled. He had a charming smile.

Dander high, not thinking clearly, Corky tore into the

reporter. "There've been homicides here, dammit, so you get the hell away!"

"Easy now," Emil advised, leaning on his cane.

Casually, Riley crossed his wrists and held out his hands. "I'm ready for the cuffs. It'll make a damn good story, Sheriff."

"Come on," Emil said.

Corky turned away from the reporter, trying to suppress his fury. An icy wind shuddered in off Tufo's lake, but Corky's face was hot, beet-red. "You been inside yet?" he demanded of Deputy Gosch.

"No, Sheriff. I did like you told me, just guarded the house. Deputy Poll and Bawlie Wepner are out hunting for Josh Miggs, one of Trixie's boys. The live one. Bawlie found him in the bakery truck, took him into his house. But then he ran away."

"Which way?"

"Across the lake and into the trees."

"You see the kid run out of Bawlie's house?"

"Nope. I didn't see nothin' until this here reporter showed up in his van."

"Good work," said Corky. He studied the yellow house thoughtfully.

"One of us has got to go in," Emil said.

Corky interpreted this remark as a rebuke, which Emil had not intended it to be. Emil remembered all too well the fear, confusion, and false hopes on that hot August night Reverend Matthew Koster had killed his family. He remembered, and would remember until the end of his days, the eerie feeling he had experienced upon entering that house of death.

"I'll go in," Corky declared. "I'm not afraid." He unsnapped his holster and took out the black .45 caliber pistol. "Gosch, get your weapon out, we're going in."

Shakily, Jamie unholstered his weapon and checked the chamber. "Safety off, Sheriff?"

"Safety off."

Corky advanced on the door, then turned. "Emil, you think somebody might still be in there?"

"Send Gosch around to the back door," Emil said quickly. He noticed that Roy Riley had pulled a notepad out of his pocket and was shorthanding energetically. Corky, just do something! he thought. When you read about yourself in the *Trib*, you're not going to be too happy.

The sheriff took Emil's advice, sent Jamie around to the back. Pausing for a deep breath, he tried the doorknob. It turned easily in his hand. Giving Whippletree a forlorn glance, Corky slid into the house, .45 upraised, free hand extended as if he were balancing on a wire.

"So you're Emil Whippletree!" Roy Riley exuded, offering his hand enthusiastically. "Since I came to Stearns County, everyone has told me you're the guy I should meet."

"I haven't the slightest idea why," Emil replied, shaking Riley's hard hand, mindful of Corky's warning not to start talking too much.

"You're a big hero in these parts, Sheriff. You know that?"

"Oh, I doubt it."

"No, it's true. You solved the Koster case. Want to talk about it?"

"I wasn't a big hero while I was working on that case. I got reamed, steamed, and dry-cleaned by the *Tribune.*"

"Yo!" called Gosch, from the rear of the Miggs house. "All clear here!"

"Yeah, but you solved it."

Emil shrugged. "I'd rather forget the whole thing. Matthew Koster shot his wife and four kids. He was in love with another woman, and he was a minister. I guess he figured he had to be free of them before she would see him as a serious suitor. He thought in absolutes."

"I can see that," Riley observed. "Death is pretty absolute. Yet nobody believed a clergyman would kill. Why did you?"

"I didn't at first. But that's the way it turned out." He decided to end the post-mortem. "Why did you come up here from Chicago?" he asked.

"I was sick of big-city corruption," Riley said.

Corky Withers came hurtling out of the Miggs house, the pistol still in his hand, his other hand jammed to his mouth. The wide-brimmed sheriff's hat fell off and fluttered to the hard-packed snow of the Miggs' driveway as Corky raced around the corner of the garage, where he upchucked violently on some pine shrubbery.

Emil saw Roy Riley writing on his notepad.

Deputy Gosch came around the corner of the house. "What the hell is going on? Where's Corky? I was waitin' for him to call me in." He heard the last of the sound effects from around the corner, saw the open door and Corky's hat lying on the snow. "Guess it's bad, huh?"

Corky returned, wiping his mouth with a white handkerchief. He picked up his hat and jammed it onto his head, looking embarrassed. Whippletree noticed a flicker of sympathy cross Roy Riley's broad, cynical face, and made a private judgment in the reporter's favor.

Corky struggled to find words for what he'd seen in the house.

Emil looked down through the trees and onto the lake, hoping for a glimpse of Poll or Wepner or the runaway kid. A thin, wavery tendril of smoke rose from the tin chimney of Nubs Tufo's cabin. That might mean Nubs had banked his fire and gone out to check his traps. Nubs made his living these days from muskrat, mink, and weasel plus a monthly social security check.

"Corky, what's in the house?" Emil demanded.

"Somebody who's dead."

"One body?"

"That's all I saw—before I had to come out."

"Woman or child?"

"I couldn't tell."

"That bad?"

Corky nodded.

"We've got to go in," Emil said. "Jamie, you go around to the back again, just in case."

Whippletree limped toward the door. Roy Riley scribbled. Corky hurried to reach the house first.

The furnace was running and the house was warm. Whippletree smelled blood.

The front door opened into a small living room, fairly neat, with a beige wall-to-wall carpet, two easy chairs, and a couch. Shades were pulled down over the windows.

Standing just inside the door, thinking, Whippletree noticed Roy Riley next to him, still taking notes. Well, he would let Corky Withers worry about the reporter. His attention was already engaged by the house, by the *feel* of the house, and what that feeling might be able to tell him.

Corky led the way through the living room. Emil followed. Roy Riley brought up the rear. The presence of death was more pronounced with each step toward the back of the house. There was only one floor, with the living and dining rooms in front, kitchen and garage off to one side, darkened bedrooms toward the back. Emil saw Corky swallow hard, brace himself, and turn toward the kitchen. Corky paused in the kitchen doorway and unsuccessfully fought down an impulse to retch.

Emil had never been in a war, but no one as old as he was, who had grown up in this country when it had been raw frontier, was a stranger to blood. Arms ground to pulp by corn pickers. Legs gouged and sliced by misswung axes. The crushed, battered bodies of those who had fallen from barns or silos. Emil had seen and tried to assuage the pain of all these things.

But not even in the Koster house, bad as that sight had been, had he seen a horror like the Miggs kitchen.

The body was seated upright in a chair at the kitchen table, which was littered with beer bottles—ten of them—and the silver trays of three partially eaten TV dinners. A bag of taco chips, barbeque flavored, spilled over the edge of the table and onto the floor. They had been powdered underfoot. There was an empty Pepsi bottle on the floor, and another on the table. An ashtray in front of the body was filled with butts, and two cigarettes remained in the crushed pack of Salems next to the ashtray. The victim was a woman, dressed in a loose-fitting flannel robe and a cotton nightgown drooping low over her full breasts. Breasts, cut of clothes, and delicate, long-fingered hands attested to femininity. That was all.

Because the body was headless.

"Yo!" hollered Deputy Gosch, outside the back door, "everything's fine here."

"Good," Corky quavered, in a high-pitched voice, "just stay there. Any sign of Wepner or Poll?"

"Nope."

Whippletree stood just inside the kitchen doorway, scanning the room, taking in everything he could and trying to store it in memory. Several days worth of unwashed dishes were in the sink and on the counter beside the sink. The top of the refrigerator was gray with dust. He'd once been six-two—old age had wreaked about an inch of shrinkage—but he could see the top of the fridge all right. A calendar, taped to the refrigerator door, was still open to November, the month illustrated by a canvasback in flight, one feather falling from a wing. The blasted, blood-spattered clock on the wall behind the victim said 4:22.

Emil caned his way slowly into the room, and felt beneath the rubber tip of his cane and under the soles of his boots the slippery roll of buckshot. The floor was littered with it. Since his knee wouldn't permit him to bend down, he asked Corky to give him a few of the pellets. Rolling them between his fingers, Whippletree shook his head.

"What is it?" Riley asked.

"More than just murder. Whoever did this wanted Trixie Miggs blown off the face of the earth. Probably used a double-barreled shotgun, most likely eight-gauge, maybe ten, and fired it at her head four times, maybe six, until the head was gone." He took a breath and swallowed. "It would have been like loading a steel pipe with nails and dynamite and setting it off in somebody's mouth.

"Corky," he asked. "Have you called the lab boys from State Bureau of Criminal Apprehension?"

"Right, Emil. They're supposed to be on their way."

"Good. Every inch of this house'll have to be dusted. Don't touch anything. Let's check in the back."

Corky led the way to the opposite side of the little house and into a darkened bedroom, switching on the light.

"Don't touch anything!" Emil repeated.

This bedroom had belonged to Trixie Miggs. It smelled of stale laundry and perfume more powerful than Corky's lemon-lime. The bed was unmade, a frilly but faded coverlet thrown back, blankets and sheets in disarray. It was a double bed. Both pillows were bunched and crumpled. A pair of blue jeans had been tossed across the back of a wooden chair next to the bed, along with a white blouse and a red bra. A pair of matching panties lay on the floor next to the chair. There was no rug. An unpainted dresser stood against the wall at the foot of the bed, with combs, brushes, curlers, lotions, perfumes, and a little statue of the Blessed Virgin on top of the dresser. The closet door was open and Whippletree looked inside. Mrs. Miggs had been partial to blue jeans and cowboy boots. A bulging laundry bag sagged from a hook on the door.

"The other bedroom's just over here," said Riley, from the doorway.

"Yo!" called Gosch, still outside, "You guys all right in there?"

"Yeah," shouted Corky, "we'll be out in a minute."

The other bedroom was not empty. Corky flicked the light switch carefully this time with the edge of a fingernail. The window shade was drawn, as it had been in Mrs. Miggs' room, and a bare electric light bulb on the ceiling cut the gloom and showed two mattresses on the floor and a gun-blasted sleeping bag on top of each. One sleeping bag was unzipped and unoccupied, but in the other lay the body of a tow-headed boy, about ten years of age, Whippletree reckoned. He had been shot in the abdomen, now a bloody crater of rent fabric and torn organs. His eyes were slightly open.

"He never knew what hit him." Whippletree closed the child's eyes.

"This is—was Roger," observed Sheriff Withers. He looked at the second sleeping bag. "I wonder how Josh got out?"

Roy Riley was taking notes.

"I guess we'll have to ask Josh," Whippletree figured, "if we ever find him. Say, Corky—I mean Sheriff—when did Bawlie Wepner phone your office to report finding Josh in his bread truck?"

They had left the bedroom and were walking back toward the front door.

Corky shrugged and checked his watch. It was almost ten now. "I guess it was about seven-thirty, quarter to eight."

Whippletree looked into the kitchen again, at the terrible wall on which the ruined clock read 4:22. The wall looked as if some insane artist had hurled against it first a bucket of red dye, then a container full of gray paste, and lastly a handful of snarled cornsilk. Like a representative Minnesotan, Trixie Miggs had been a blonde.

"Wonder what Josh Miggs did from roughly four-thirty

till seven-thirty," Emil drawled. "Why didn't he run to Bawlie's place and bang on his door? Or even go over to Nubs' cabin by the lake?"

"Corky, if a kid were to run outside in his pajamas in this kind of weather, what are the chances he'd survive three hours? If he was in a freezing cold bread truck or not?" Riley asked.

Corky thought it over. "That's it!" he exclaimed.

"What is?" asked Riley.

"This case is solved!" Corky exulted. "Don't you see? Josh Miggs is the killer. It's clear as a bell now, isn't it, Emil? The kid killed his mother and brother, for reasons we don't know yet. He couldn't walk out of here, too young to drive, so he hid out in Wepner's truck, waiting to get a free lift to St. Cloud. Then, when he found out I'd be coming, he got scared and ran off."

"Maybe," Whippletree said, "Maybe. But what's in St. Cloud? Why would he want to go there?"

"The railroad. The bus."

"Where to?"

"Anywhere. *Out*. People run when they have to."

"I think he has, and it was only into the woods," Emil said.

He and Corky and the reporter went outside. The cold air was as strong as ammonia for a moment, after the stench of the Miggs house.

"Is that you guys?" hollered Gosch. He came running around the corner of the house, gun drawn and ready. "It is you guys," he said, relieved. "What's inside?"

"Two bodies," Corky told him.

Emil drew Corky off to the side. "How come you didn't call me until after nine, if Bawlie Wepner was already on the horn to you before eight A.M.?"

Corky looked away. "I got Gosch and Poll out here to secure the site," he managed. "I got the site secured, anyway." Then, with difficulty, he met Emil's eyes. "I had to *think* a little. I had to figure out what to do."

The old sheriff resisted an impulse to say, *so you called me*. "I doubt it's the kid," he said instead.

"How do you know?"

Emil shook his head. "I can't tell you, but I just know."

Corky looked crestfallen. He had already solved the case in his imagination, had seen a big victorious headline in the *Tribune*.

"You're going to have to eat some dirt from that reporter, I hope you know."

"That outsider sonofabitch," Corky responded, glaring at the black Dodge van to which Roy Riley had retreated. "He's probably sending dispatches to St. Paul."

"No, he's probably just trying to keep warm. Listen to me. You've got a big job and lots of authority. But if you don't know how to do the job or use the authority, then you might as well go back to baling hay."

"Heeee-eyyy!" The call came from across Tufo's lake, echoed upon the stand of trees along the shore. "Heee-eyyy."

Whippletree turned and saw two figures coming over the ice toward the murder house. They were still a considerable distance away. The lake was not particularly large, but it was big enough. Minnesota, which advertised itself as the "Land of 10,000 Lakes," defined a lake as any body of water covering ten acres or more. There were over twelve thousand lakes according to that criterion, and thousands upon thousands of smaller ponds. Tufo's lake was just a little bigger than a pond.

"It's Poll," Corky said, as the men came closer. "And Bawlie Wepner."

"Yep. And they're alone."

"Hey, Emil!" called Poll, trudging up from the frozen lake. He was a chunky, aging kid, who had once been a local football star.

Bawlie Wepner came up behind Poll. He was panting

slightly. Liquor had thickened his face and his middle, but he was solid, not fat, and in better shape than Poll. Bawlie looked pretty worried. He nodded to Emil in perfunctory greeting, then turned to Corky Withers.

"Sheriff, I'm sorry, but I just don't know how it happened. Me an' Poll was drinking coffee over at my place, the kid was watching TV. We was waitin' for you to get here, and no sooner do we turn around than the kid is gone."

Roy Riley clambered out of his warm van and came over, notepad at the ready.

"Watch what you say, everybody," warned Corky. "Mr. Wepner, I'm not blaming you," he said, glaring at Poll. "What was the boy wearing?"

"Hell, I don't know. Windbreaker. Pair of shoes . . . "

"Boots?" asked Whippletree. "Heavy coat?"

"Naw. Just shoes. And a hat. He had him on a stocking hat, like skiers wear."

Josh's choice of apparel didn't make sense, thought Emil, not if the boy figured to get far in weather like this. But he hadn't fled the house in pajamas *only*, which suggested an absence of acute panic.

"All right," said Corky, in a take-charge voice that was only a little tentative, "I'll radio the office and tell Deputy Vogel to get a search party up. Also, we'll need Doc Divot, the county coroner, out here. He can liaise with the state BCA team, whenever they show up, and I hope it's soon. What do we need to haul the bodies out, Emil? Ambulance or hearse?"

"Ambulance. Divot'll do the autopsies before there's any need for a funeral home."

"O-*kay!*" Corky said, in a let's-get-cracking tone.

Roy Riley raised his hand. "Question, Sheriff Withers."

"Yeah? What?"

"Is Josh Miggs old enough to drive?"

"What? What has that got to do with anything?"

"I note that there's a garage here, and no one's looked into it."

So they did. Deputy Gosch rolled up the door. One of the rollers went off its metal track, and the lowest panel of the rickety garage door flapped loose on one side, like a wooden bird with a bad wing. The garage was narrow, smelled of grease, and held one Plymouth Duster, vintage 1969.

"Good luck on those snow tires," Poll said. "They're as bald as my mother-in-law's ass."

"How would you know?" Gosch asked.

"Cut the crap," said Corky.

Emil edged into the garage, alongside the old car. The key was in the ignition. He opened the door and slid onto the freezing upholstery, keeping his bad leg outside the car. Turning the ignition key produced a faint, fleeting whine, and then nothing.

"Emil, the fingerprints on the key!" screamed Corky.

Whippletree waved his handkerchief. "Used edges of the key only. And this baby's battery is dead as hell. Without a power jump, nobody could've gone anywhere in it."

"Trixie Miggs got a jump yesterday," Bawlie observed, as Emil came out of the frigid concrete garage. "And the day before."

"Who from?" asked Corky.

"Don't know. Some guy in a green GMC pickup."

Roy Riley looked at him. "You seem to have kept a pretty good eye on the deceased?"

"She was a damn good-looking woman." Bawlie Wepner scowled, moving his shoulders a little to show the reporter that he could handle himself. "*I* would notice something like that."

"Especially since you live alone way out here."

Wepner took a step toward the reporter, then realized how a show of violence might be interpreted.

"I'm just a neighbor," he said. "I'm sorry as hell about what happened."

"Yeah," said Riley.

Corky Withers snapped his fingers. "Oh, Jesus!"

"Yeah, Sheriff?"

"Here we're standing around and—and they got to get last rites. I completely forgot."

Everyone nodded somberly. Extreme unction was a right of the dead.

"Who's the nearest priest?" Corky asked.

"Father Peter Creedmore, pastor in Silverton," Emil said. "He ought to be able to get here in a couple of minutes."

"Mr. Wepner, can I use your phone?" Corky asked.

Bawlie, who had not been called 'mister' too often in his whole life, managed to nod. Corky dog-trotted toward the Wepner house.

Whippletree remembered that Florence Hockapuk, Sarah's opponent in the Rosary Society election, was a staunch member of Father Creedmore's Life Saviors, Stearns County's branch of the national Right-to-Life movement.

"Can I use your phone too, Bawlie?" Whippletree asked. "Got to give Sarah a call or she'll think I've hit the ditch somewhere."

"Sure thing, Emil."

Whippletree began to cane down the Miggs' driveway, heading toward Bawlie's house.

Roy Riley motioned him toward the van. "Hey, Sheriff. Come in here and warm up."

"But I've got to phone—"

"Come in here!" Riley demanded, with a glance at Wepner and the deputies. They were busy lighting cigarettes.

Riley threw open the back door of the van, touched a button. A short rise of metal steps slid out of the vehicle's body. Whippletree braced himself with the cane and prepared to climb into the van, but then he stopped, amazed at the vehicle's interior. Just after retirement, he and Sarah had flown to Hawaii on vacation. The cockpit door of the plane had been open as they boarded and Emil had gotten a glimpse of the ship's bridge, with its fantastic array of gauges and dials and lights. Subtract a pilot's yoke, add what appeared to be a small waterbed, and Riley's van presented a fair approximation of a jetliner's cockpit.

" 'Star Trek.' " Emil shrugged, making it up and into the van.

Riley laughed and closed the door. Emil sat down on the bed. There was liquid in it, all right. "Looks like you got everything in here but the kitchen sink."

"Oh, that's here." Riley pointed. "Behind the black panel. I don't have the encryption, though. You know, a scrambler for radio traffic, that Sheriff Withers wishes he had? I don't have a satellite dish either, although I'm working on that. What's your home telephone number?"

"What?"

"Your number? I thought you wanted to call your wife."

Whippletree gave him the number, and Riley pressed keys on a console that resembled a typewriter but wasn't. The sound of a ringing phone, origin indeterminate, filled the van, followed by Sarah's tentative "Hello?"

Emil was so amazed that he didn't think to speak right away.

"Hello?" Sarah asked again, more firmly.

"Ah . . . it's me."

"Emil! Are you all right? You sound funny."

"No, I'm fine. Really. I don't know when I'll be home, though. That's what I'm calling to say."

"Is Father Creedmore there yet?" she asked.

Riley and Whippletree exchanged glances.

"Sarah, why do you think Father Creedmore's coming here?"

"I just got that call I was expecting from Sister Terence. She was at the Chancery office. Father Creedmore phoned Bishop Bundeswehr to say he'd be gone from his rectory for awhile because he had to give last rites to those people who'd been shot. Bishop told Sister and she told me."

Whippletree suppressed a sigh. So the word was out now, for sure, from Corky to Creedmore to "Imperial Bill" Bundeswehr to Sister Terence and God alone knew who else. By evening, the Miggs murders would be meat for supper-table jabber from St. Alois in the east to St. Rupert in the west and all the other St. this-or-thats in between.

Naturally, news of the killings would get out anyway— Riley would do a story for tomorrow's *Tribune*—but Emil felt that, somehow, he could trust the reporter to handle the matter responsibly. If gossip spread the news first, however, Corky was going to be up against the kind of situation Emil had had to face during the Koster case: a storm of bizarre rumors, each more fantastic than the last.

Emil debated going straight to Wilhelm Bundeswehr and asking his help in keeping the lid on. "Imperial Bill," whose nickname had been earned by taste in automobiles as well as the character of his reign, was Stearns County's pre-eminent public figure.

"Emil, how bad is it out there?" Sarah was asking.

"I don't want to talk about it now. See you later."

"Emil, wait! Hugh called from Iowa. He and Dory plan to arrive sometime on the afternoon of Christmas Eve."

Hugh was Emil's younger brother, now a lawyer in Dubuque, and Dory was his wife. Emil had put Hugh through law school years ago, even though he'd been pretty damned hard up at the time. But he hadn't wanted to see his kid brother succumb to the Stearns County Syndrome.

"I hope it doesn't snow and block the highways," Emil said. He always looked forward to seeing Hugh.

"I'll light a candle," Sarah said.

"That'll do it. 'Bye."

" 'Bye." Sarah hung up the phone in St. Cloud and the receiver's click resounded in the van.

Riley slid aside a panel to reveal a small galley and a Mr. Coffee machine. He filled a cup. "Sugar? Milk?"

"Black, thanks. How'd you do that with the phone?"

"Easy." Riley handed Emil the coffee, and sat down on a stool next to the galley. "Patched right into the line. Don't worry. It's all legal."

Emil sipped the hot coffee. It tasted damn good. "Corky'd have a fit if he knew the gear you've got in here."

Slowly, Riley lit a Salem, took a deep drag. "Sheriff, don't you think Corky is too naïve to figure out something as complicated as a murder case?" He smiled, and his hard, round face lost its cynicism.

"Learned stuff like that down there in Chicago, did you?"

"I want to get away from what I learned there."

"You came out here to the sticks to enjoy a nice place with good people?"

"Right. Don't have to lock your door at night."

"Until now," Emil said.

The coffee was cooler, and Whippletree took a long swallow, looking out the van window at Tufo's Lake. He glanced at his watch. The kid would freeze.

Then he saw, down in the stripped, gray bushes where Zorn Creek ran out of the lake, a shadowy movement behind branches. Even at this distance, Emil could see the bushes shiver.

"What is it, Emil?" Riley asked, turning to look as well.

"Don't know . . ."

A shape, dark and large, larger than a man, loomed for an instant amid the leafless stand of brush along the shore.

The size, the nature of the movement, reminded Emil of a bear, but there were no bears around here any more. Then the bushes parted and a dark-coated figure moved out onto the lake. Emil saw why the figure had seemed bigger than a man. He grabbed the cane and struggled to his feet.

"It's Nubs Tufo and he's got the Miggs boy over his shoulder."

3

Norbert J. "Nubs" Tufo didn't say much. Never had. Hadn't had to in the old days, farming; didn't need to these days, trapping; and didn't want to anyway. Words caused almost as much trouble as people did. Emil had often thought that if everybody in the county were transported a century backward into time, if they had to settle and tame the land as their ancestors had done, Nubs would be one of the few to survive. Although he wouldn't think to brag the fact, Emil reckoned he'd be standing among that number too.

Corky Withers came running out of Bawlie's house just as Emil descended shakily from Riley's van.

"That's Nubs coming across the lake," Emil shouted to the young sheriff. "He's got the Miggs kid."

Corky appraised the situation and, to his credit, acted fast.

"Poll, Gosch! Get in the car!"

The sheriff and his two deputies piled into the patrol car, jounced over ice-hardened drifts and onto the lake. Emil leaned on his cane and watched as the car approached Nubs, and stopped. Corky got out, looked at the Miggs boy, and ordered him transferred from Nubs' big shoulders to the backseat of the car.

"Hope the kid's okay," Riley said.

Then the car, with Gosch, Poll and Josh Miggs in it, came back across Tufo's Lake, struggled up through the trees, wheels spinning, and shot off toward Silverton and St. Cloud. Jittery Jamie was driving. Poll was in the backseat with Josh Miggs. He looked worried and covered the boy with his storm coat. The car sped out of sight.

Nubs and Corky came off the lake and up the bank.

"The kid looks in a real bad way," Corky said. "What's it called? Hyperthermalon?"

"Hypothermia," Riley corrected.

"Hope he makes it," Corky worried. "He's our only witness, as far as we know."

"I found him way down the creek," Nubs put in, "huddled up at the base of a tree, right near the location of one of my muskrat traps. He was out cold."

"Poor kid," Riley said.

"Hey, Emil," grunted Nubs. He offered a mittened hand. "Surprised to see you here." He grinned, displaying tobacco-stained teeth.

Emil had last seen Nubs at the Fourth of July Sportsmen's Bazaar. In his thick padded woodsman's coat, he looked sturdy and strong as ever. He carried a .22 caliber rifle. Four muskrat, sleek and dead, hung from his belt. Each of the animals had a leg mangled by a steel trap, and the leg of one was almost severed where the muskrat had tried to chew it off to escape, an unsuccessful effort since Nubs had arrived in time to put a .22 bullet in its brain. Only Roy Riley, city boy, felt anything approaching sorrow for the animals. To Corky and Emil and Nubs, a muskrat existed to be trapped and made into somebody's fur coat.

"What the hell is going on here?" Nubs asked, looking at the men and gesturing toward the Miggs house with the barrel of his .22 rifle.

"Somebody shot Trixie and one of her kids," said Bawlie Wepner, coming out from behind a tree and zipping up his fly.

Nubs received this information, frowned, and looked at the house again. "Hell, I ain't too damn surprised," he rasped.

"Why's that?" Roy Riley asked.

"Shut up," Corky told him. "I ask the questions here. "Why's that, Mr. Tufo?"

Nubs gave him a measuring look. "You're the new sheriff? I seen your picture in the *Trib* a time or two."

Emil knew Nubs pretty well, and he saw that the old man was not about to tell young Corky much of anything.

"Didn't happen to see anything unusual around here lately, did you, Nubs?" Emil drawled, trying to make it casual.

"Them Miggs' is *all* unusual. Or was."

"What?"

"Boys always fighting with each other, troublemakers. Mother hooring around. But," he shrugged, "when I saw that kid freezing to death under the tree, I just had to pick him up and carry him out."

"This is very, *very* important," said Corky, trying again. "Have you seen anyone suspicious around here lately? Like last night, in particular?"

Nubs gave him a long stare, then looked at Emil and jerked his head in the direction of Roy Riley's van. Nubs walked behind the van, out of the wind, and Emil followed him slowly.

"What's the matter with your leg, Emil? You got the gout, or what?"

The doc had told Emil this would happen. "Practice saying osteoarthritis," Doc had advised, "or everybody's gonna rib you about gout."

"Rheumatism," said Emil.

"Shit, I saved you from drowning your rear end all those years ago just so you could go and get pitiful in your old age? Ought to come over to my place. Have some brandy or whip up a batch of Tom and Jerries. It's the Christmas season, so says the man on the radio. Now, what's going on here?"

"Trixie Miggs and her kid were shotgunned. Maybe

Josh did it, maybe not. Seen anyone around here lately?"

"Just between the two of us?"

"Nubs, I can't warranty that. It's a murder."

"I thought you was retired."

"I am. But Corky called me. He needs help."

Nubs shook his head. "You ain't whistling Dixie on that one. Anyway, yeah, I have seen some stuff. But I don't want to read my name in the gottdamn papers. The guy who owns this van is that new reporter, ain't he?"

"He is. But I think he's okay. That's my personal judgment."

"Shit, Emil, you always was too trusting a guy, that was always your big problem. But I'll tell you what I seen, past couple of days. Main thing, there's this guy with a green GMC pickup. Always coming around. Like Trixie Miggs is a bitch in heat."

"Know who he is?"

"Nope. But the bastard tried to dump some garbage on my property, couple of days ago."

"What happened?"

"I made him pick it up and put it back on his truck. Threatened to sic my dog, Stormy, on him." Nubs looked disgusted, even sad. "And then her husband comes around now and then, too. Or her ex-husband. Whatever the hell the situation is."

"Know him?"

"Not much. Felix is his name. They call him Flinch. Was working as a security guard at the Crossroads shopping center. She kicked him out, or he run out on her, about a year ago."

It didn't take Emil long to figure that a security guard always had access to a weapon.

"Why do they call him Flinch?"

Nubs helped himself to a chaw of Copenhagen and shook his head derisively. "Because when he gets drunk at the Goose Step Inn there in Silverton, he'll tell guys to punch him in the mouth. 'I'm a better man than anybody,' he tells them, 'I won't flinch.' "

"What happens?"

"He always flinches."

"Good Lord," said Emil. In barn-dance days of yore, guys tried to punch through the walls of the barn. These days they snowmobiled from a tavern in one town to a tavern in another, looking for fights.

"I got the license number of the GMC," Nubs was saying. "Over in my cabin. I wrote it down. Habit I got into the past couple years, with so many asshole trespassers from them terrific Twin Cities wanting to hunt on my land. What time did you say Trixie was shot?"

"Along about four A.M." Emil spat tobacco juice. So did Nubs.

"You're kiddin'?" Nubs said.

"About what?"

"Four A.M. There was a car in Trixie's driveway at just about that time. I got the license number on 'er. I don't sleep too good any more."

Emil nodded. He didn't sleep too well either, these days. Age.

"Well, there was a good moon, so I thought I'd set out early to run my trap line. I'm set up all along Zorn Creek for miles, takes me all morning to check. Anyway, I left the cabin and saw a car up here. Just sittin' there in the driveway. So I come across the lake, saw it real good. The driver must have seen me comin', on account of he backed out and drove away. Seemed funny to me, so I memorized the license number, went back and wrote it down."

Emil felt excited. "What make of car?"

"Hell, I don't know. They all look alike to me since they don't make 'em with tailfins any more."

Then you're sure it was around four?"

"Yep. Thereabouts or a little later." Nubs shivered. "I'm

going back to my place, have a brandy and warm up. I want to live through another Christmas, anyway. Come on over and I'll give you them numbers."

Nubs hitched up his belt, and the muskrat carcasses turned and shifted against his thigh. "One other thing, an' you didn't hear this from me."

"You got it."

"Bawlie Wepner's been in that house to see Trixie a time or two hisself."

"Bawlie?"

"You better believe it."

Nubs spat some more tobacco juice, and set out for his cabin.

Emil caned back to Corky, Bawlie, and Roy Riley, who were all shuffling around, backs hunched against the wind.

"What'd he want?" Corky asked resentfully.

Just then a Chrysler LeBaron, pretty new, came speeding up the road. The car slowed a bit, approaching Bawlie's house, then braked, skidded slightly, and turned into the Miggs' driveway.

"It's Father Creedmore, here to give last rites," Corky said.

Emil had seen Father Peter Creedmore's picture in the *Trib* many times. The priest stared with intense, piercing black eyes from news photos, with an expression of mournful commitment.

In person, Peter Creedmore looked just like he did in his pictures, but the impression he gave was subtly different. He seemed more and less than the sum of his reputation. When he got out of the LeBaron, Whippletree saw a powerful, barrel-chested man with hair the color and texture of a Brillo pad. Creedmore wore a black suit, no topcoat, his only concession to the bitter weather a gray woolen scarf wrapped loosely around his thick neck. He had a brawler's build, but the black eyes of those *Trib* photos evaded Emil's gaze, slid off the greeting glances of the other men, and when he said, "Gentlemen, this is a sad day," his voice was soft and almost indistinct.

Yet, when he strode toward the yellow house, carrying the black Extreme Unction kit with its holy water and holy oil, candles and crucifix, there was not a doubt in the world that he knew exactly who he was and what he had been called here to do. Whippletree and the others followed him to the door. Emil noticed, as the priest reached out for the doorknob, an expensive Rollex and a thick rubber band on a hairy wrist.

Father Peter Creedmore entered the house.

"Corky, go with him," Emil suggested. "Make sure nothing is touched or disturbed."

Corky nodded and went inside, struggling a little to pull the storm door shut against a rising wind.

"You guys want to come in my van?" Riley offered. "It's nice and warm in there. Coffee, too."

"Don't mind if I do," Bawlie Wepner said, pounding his gloved hands together, stamping his feet.

Riley, Bawlie, and Emil were heading toward the van when Emil observed a black Ford coming up the road from the direction of Silverton.

"It's the state boys," he said. "Bet they're happy as hell, having to drive all the way up from The Cities today."

"Well, the BCA's here before Doc Divot," Bawlie said.

The Ford came to a halt next to Father Creedmore's LeBaron. Two men got out, both wearing baggy business suits. Whippletree recognized one of them, the driver, and was recognized in turn.

"Hey, Sheriff, I heard you retired," said Jiggsy Potoff. He reached into the backseat of the Ford, snatched an overcoat and put it on, came over and shook Emil's hand. "This here's my partner, Leander Fruth. Leander's one of our forensic men. Get your coat on, Leander."

Leander shook hands with Emil, then with Wepner and Riley. Emil made the introductions.

"I'm retired, all right," he said. "I kind of got pressed

into duty. Sheriff Withers is in the house now with a priest, who's giving last rites."

"Hope he doesn't disturb any evidence," Fruth said. "What's the exact story, and when did the killings occur?"

"Don't know much for sure, except time of death was four twenty-two this morning. Shattered clock."

Father Creedmore came out of the house then and strode, head down, to his car, neither looking at nor speaking to the men standing in the driveway. In less than half a minute, he had gotten into the LeBaron, started it up, backed out of the driveway and sped off. No good-bye wave. Whippletree had a funny feeling.

He did not have time to analyze it, though, because Corky, who'd followed Creedmore out of the house, came over to be introduced to the state team. Corky looked bewildered.

"Everything go all right in there?" Emil asked him, trying to keep a trace of anxiety out of his voice.

"Oh, sure, you bet," affirmed Corky.

Emil introduced Potoff and Fruth.

"So you're the new sheriff," Potoff said. "You have a great predecessor. Well, Leander, let's get in there and get to work so the coroner can remove the bodies for autopsy."

"There's ah, there's just one thing," said Corky hesitantly.

Potoff looked at him. "Yes?"

"There's no way—what I mean is—what I—well, this won't be in the—on TV in The Cities, will it? Or in the papers there?"

Potoff looked at Corky more closely. "Can't say it won't. In fact, good chance it will. I'd think, if you solved the case quick, that it might do you some good."

"Well, I'll—ah—we'll solve it, all right. It's just that I'd rather—ah, keep it under wraps for the time being," Corky was saying. "You understand?"

Jiggsy Potoff shrugged. "I can't guarantee nothin'," he said. "Come on, Leander. You got the camera?"

"When Father Creedmore entered the house and viewed the bodies," asked Riley, pencil poised, "what was his reaction?"

"Aw, shut up," replied Corky, in a tone that was almost despondent. "Emil, can I see you for a sec?"

Corky and Emil climbed into the sheriff's car. Corky started the engine, gunned it. A tremendous blast of frigid air came out of the heating ducts and then, slowly, the car began to warm up.

Roy Riley gave the two of them a wave, climbed into his Dodge van, and drove off.

"God, we need a scrambler," Corky mourned. "You were in the van. What's he got in there?"

"Plenty. But why do you need a scrambler, really?"

"Why, to keep Riley from finding out what's going on!"

"He certainly didn't need a scrambler today," Emil allowed drily. "All he had to do was stand around with his eyes and ears half open."

"Jeez, I guess so," Corky said. "Emil, I think we've got another problem. When I was in the house with Father Creedmore? When he was giving last rites?"

Whippletree had sensed that something had gone wrong inside the house. "Yes?"

"Father—ah, well, he sort of moved a few things— moved them around."

"What things?"

"Like—ah, the bodies."

"The bodies!" Emil cried. "Why in the hell did you— why did you let him? What was in your head, anyway?"

"Emil, Father Creedmore's a *priest!* He was performing a *sacrament!* I just didn't feel I had the right to tell him what to do and what not to do."

"Well," sighed Emil, "how did he move them?"

"He laid Mrs. Miggs on the kitchen floor. And he made

me take the boy out of the sleeping bag and put him on the other mattress. Had to anoint the kid's feet, you know."

That didn't sound too bad to Emil, although it was a gross violation of procedure. "We can remember where the bodies were," he said. "Look, when the BCA develops its pictures, think you can send a set over to my house?"

"Sure, Emil. You got 'em."

"Father Creedmore didn't touch a whole lot of other things in the house, did he?"

"I don't think so. I didn't notice."

"I hope not."

"But the funny thing was, after he'd anointed Roger Miggs, coming back from the kid's room, he went into Mrs. Miggs' bedroom for a minute. I was walking ahead of him, I turned around, he wasn't there. He was in her bedroom."

"What for?"

"I don't know."

"Corky, when you left the kitchen and went back to the boy's room, who led the way?"

"Why . . . let's see . . . Father Creedmore did."

"Did he go directly there? Did he glance into the master bedroom when he walked past it?"

"I don't get you, Emil."

"He knew the house. He'd been in it before."

"Oh, hell, Emil. That doesn't mean anything. The Miggses belong to Creedmore's parish in Silverton. He could have been here any number of times for a lot of reasons. Trixie was separated from her husband. Maybe Father Pete was called out there for advice, or something."

"You're right." Emil dropped the subject. "By the way, I think I've got good news."

"I could stand it."

"Nubs Tufo's got the license numbers of two vehicles

that have been around here lately. And one of those vehicles was here at around four this morning."

Corky twitched as if he'd just gulped a shotglass full of adrenaline. "Emil, don't kid me like that."

"Drive across the ice to Nubs' cabin and we'll pick up those numbers and call them in to the Bureau of Motor Vehicles."

"Emil, this is terrific." Corky put the car in gear, jounced down the snowy embankment and onto the lake. Excited, he accelerated too much at first and the car fishtailed on the slick ice. Then he calmed down, and crept over to the cabin.

Corky eased the car to a stop at lakeside and Nubs emerged from his cabin, leaving the door ajar, and came down a narrow, trampled pathway in the snow. Watching Nubs approach, Emil had a fleeting impression that something was missing, something was incomplete about Nubs Tufo, and had been too when they'd spoken earlier. Just a wacky impulse, he decided. Nubs, bareheaded but wrapped in a woolen plaid blanket, wearing twill trousers and high felt boots, looked strong as ever.

Corky rolled down the window. "Don't know that I can ever thank you enough—" he began.

Nubs grunted, reached across the sheriff, and handed Emil a scrap of paper. "Hope these numbers'll help you out a little," he said.

"Oh, I'm sure they will," exuded Corky, "you can count on it."

"Sounds like your campaign slogan," Nubs told him. "Better get to work on them murders or you'll be driving a bread truck like Bawlie Wepner." This was a joke to Nubs. He showed his tobacco-stained teeth.

"Thanks, Nubs," Emil said. "We'll keep you posted."

"Don't forget, Emil. You drop in for some Tom and Jerries or a brandy one of these afternoons."

"Will do."

Corky could hardly wait to see the license numbers, and practically grabbed the paper from Emil's hand as soon as he crawled away from Tufo's cabin.

"Hmmmmm," he said, "truck BRN-174, car BRN-441." He reached for the radio mike on the dash. "Oh, dammit! Can Riley hear this, do you think?"

"Chances are, yes, he can. He's got more dojiggies than a space shuttle."

"Got to think of something," Corky muttered.

"Come on, Corky, what does it matter? You may have the number of the killer's vehicle in your hand, and here you are worrying about Roy Riley getting it. Two of our citizens have been killed. The murderer is loose. He—or she—might kill again."

Corky Withers looked chastened. He shaped up, flicked a switch, and spoke into the mike. "Stearns One to Home Base. Come in?"

An electronic crackle, then: "Yeah, Sheriff?" It was Alyce, once Emil's secretary, still around.

"Alyce, it's me."

"Oh, Sheriff, am I ever glad you called! The phones've been ringing off the hooks! People want to know—"

Corky cut her off. "In a minute. Put Axel Vogel on."

"He's not here."

"I thought he was organizing a search party."

"Gee, Sheriff! I mean, we all know the boy's been found."

"Well, where the hell *is* he?" Corky yelled into the radio. If he was listening, Roy Riley was certainly getting a lesson in Stearns County law enforcement.

"He's over having early lunch at the Courthouse Bar and Grill," Alyce replied. "Then he's going to buy his mom a Christmas present. It is the Christmas season, you know."

"It is working hours you know," the sheriff shot back. "All right, you'll have to do this. Got a pencil handy?"

Over the radio came the sound of rustling papers and falling objects. "Sorry, no," said Alyce. "I got a ballpoint pen, though. Is that okay?"

For the first time since his retirement, Emil Whippletree was absolutely, perfectly content not to be sheriff.

"Right Alyce. Take these numbers down. BRN-174. BRN-441. Got 'em?"

"Got 'em, Corky—I mean, Sheriff."

"Good. Now call the State Bureau of Vehicle Registration in The Cities."

"Gotcha, Sheriff. Now—oh, hold on, there's the phone again."

Corky drove off the lake, up the bank, and into the Miggs' driveway. Over the radio, in the background, Alyce was talking on the telephone. She said "yes" a lot and "yes, of course."

"*Another* call," she said, back on the radio again.

"Who's been calling? What about?"

"Everybody. People from here in town, people from out in the country. They've all heard about the murders. I don't know how. This last call was from Father Rogers at the Chancery."

Father Rogers was the latest in a long line of Bishop Bundeswehr's Diocesan chancellors. His Excellency went through chief aides like a chain saw sliced through twigs.

"What'd Father want?" Corky asked.

"He didn't want anything. He said Bishop Bundeswehr had told him to call and offer Diocesan assistance, and also to say Father Creedmore is very upset about the murders."

Not too upset to move the evidence around, Emil reflected. He was still angry about what Father Peter had done, and that Corky had let him do it.

"We're all a little upset," Corky admitted.

"And Father Rogers asked if you could go easy on Father Creedmore if you need a deposition or anything,"

Alyce continued. "He said Father Creedmore is very sensitive about life and death."

"All right, Alyce. Anything else?"

"Only the phone calls. Oh, there's another."

"Just say no comment at this time. Got it?"

"'No comment at this time,'" Alyce repeated. She ended the radio connection and went to answer the ringing phone.

"Out," said Corky into the dead mike. He hung it on its dashboard hook. "What a mess. Emil, why would I want a deposition from Father Creedmore? He just gave Extreme Unction, that's all."

"He was one of the first people inside the house. He might have noticed something we didn't. You could have asked him that informally. But now you really ought to get a sworn statement from him."

"Why?"

"Corky, it comes under the heading of Tampering With Evidence. He moved the bodies, remember?"

"Hell, Emil, I can't make a fuss about that. The Bishop's office just asked me to go easy."

"Okay, Corky. Do what you want. Just don't ask me what to do if you don't want to listen to what I say."

"Emil, I'm sorry. I guess you're right."

"Let's go in the house and see how Potoff and Fruth are doing," Emil suggested. "You can learn a lot by watching a good team at work."

4

"

● ● ● relied heavily on the advice of . . . Emil Whippletree . . ." Sarah read aloud, pulling the paper away from Emil and sitting down next to him at the kitchen table. " . . . fear that media from the Twin Cities would learn . . ."

"Not yet, anyway," Emil said. "And it's been a whole day." He noticed that his cards were hopelessly mixed up. At least he wouldn't have to finish this game of solitaire.

"Riley's story isn't going to be good for Corky," Sarah sighed, leaning back in her chair. "He's sensitive enough as it is."

"You like Corky, don't you?"

"Of course. And so do you."

"I hate to see him mess things up."

"Well, call him then. During the campaign, he promised everybody that he'd consult with you. That's one of the reasons he got elected, young as he is."

"No. I'm not going to call him. Good chance for him to stand on his own two feet. I'm not involved in this anyway."

Sarah gave him one of her searching looks. Emil didn't like them at all. They always meant she'd seen right through his little deceits.

The phone rang and Emil answered it. "I hope your wife stays happy," said a male voice, a limpid distinctive voice that made Emil's flesh crawl. The connection was broken abruptly.

"Who was it, Emil?"

"Wrong number."

The phone rang again, and Sarah jumped to answer it. "Oh, hello, Sister Terence. How nice of you to call."

Emil blocked out the chatter. He was wondering who the anonymous caller had been, and why there'd been a reference to Sarah. He was also thinking about the guns.

Yesterday morning, he and Corky had followed the state lab boys into the Miggs house. Corky'd gone on into the kitchen with Potoff and Fruth. But Emil, still wondering about Josh Miggs' choice of clothing on a sub-zero Minnesota night, checked the closet next to the front door. Jammed full of coats, jackets, overshoes, and assorted winter gear, he eased it open carefully and peered inside, parting the garments with his cane and looking all the way to the back. There, in a corner, leaned two weapons, barrels up and stocks on the floor. One was a twelve-gauge shotgun, single barrel with pump action. The other was a 30.06 hunting rifle. Whippletree was not surprised to find the weapons. While handguns were not especially popular in the county, almost every household kept rifles or shotguns handy—for rabbit, duck, or deer—and many families owned half a dozen or more such weapons as casually as they owned fly rods and fishing tackle. The opening of fishing and hunting seasons witnessed a vast migration toward the northern wilderness.

Nor was the old sheriff surprised when he sniffed the barrels of the two guns and learned that they had both been fired very recently, possibly within the past twenty-four hours. Let the state BCA boys look into that. He already knew Trixie Miggs had been destroyed by a different type of shotgun. This one, as well as the rifle, could have been used by anyone, for any number of reasons. He just didn't know which.

Sarah was still chattering away when the metal door of the mail-slot squeaked open and clanged shut. A fistful of junk mail and Christmas cards appeared on the rug by the front door. Emil lurched over without using his cane and carried the cache back to the kitchen table.

Card from Mott and Elvira Heiderscheidt. Well, from Elvira, actually. Old Mott was dying. *Too bad, got to go see old Mott.*

Card from Tanys Voorde, friend of Sarah's from the Rosary Society.

Reminder card from Crossroad Auto Supply. Emil's new Delco Energizer battery was ready for the old Chev.

Latest issue of *escape* magazine. Guide to the high life in St. Cloud. Gotta escape a long way to get to that, Whippletree thought.

Fund request from the John Bosco Society.

Fund request from something or other.

And an actual letter. No return address. Emil ripped it open.

> Dec. 21
> St. Cloud
>
> *Dear-eX shreiff,*
>   *I just*
>   *want to say you may know me. and*
>
> *you may not know me. BUT that don't matter*
>
> *becuz I know who the killer is an so do you.*
>
> *Mywife and me are familiarity with him it scares*
>
> *me to thimk he knows the layout of my house an*
>
> *when I am gone and she is there all by*
>
>   *hereself. THIS IS SERIOUS I AM NOT A NUT RITING aynimous*
>   *mail to you. I wouldn't do*
> *that becuz I am a honest man an stick up for my*
>
> *right. BUT for manyyears I have seen how this*
>
> *man is an onetime took handwriting sample*

and sent it in. It came back that
                               myfriend was
VERY distubed from his hand writing and I
believe it. Youare on the right track you beter

beleeve it. I have knon this man well an have hung

around with him an mywife. Keep up the good
work an dont let noting slow youdown.
                                 A Friend
PS DONT SHOW THIS TO NOBODY.

The right track? Whippletree thought. What the hell was going on here, anyway? If this letter had resulted from Riley's article in the paper, the writer must either know Riley or know somebody from the paper, because the postmark was yesterday. That letter was in the post office before the *Trib* had gone to press. Or else word-of-mouth—Stearns County's favorite sport—had inspired the writer. In which case, what was word-of-mouth circulating?

Or maybe "aynimous" was the phone caller, with his wimpy, limpid voice? A nut case, pure and simple.

THIS IS SERIOUS I AM NOT A NUT . . .

Emil checked to make sure Sarah wasn't looking, folded the letter and stuck it in his shirt pocket. He looked as innocent as your average felon by the time Sarah put down the phone. But she was excited, barely glancing at the mail.

"Emil, can you drive me over to Crossroads now? I need a new dress. It's all decided. The ladies will wear blue at midnight Mass, because it's Mary's color, after all. Sister Terence feels it'll be appropriate."

"Sure thing. Let's get ready."

Before dressing, Emil checked the outdoor thermometer—nice and warm today, seven degrees above zero—and decided on thermal long johns and his brown wool suit, with a white shirt, and a good tie. He was, after all, going out, and although he didn't want to let on to Sarah, it had given him quite a kick to see his name in the paper again.

He was getting into his overcoat and thinking about the letter and Roy Riley's newspaper story, when he remembered yesterday's exchange between Riley and Bawlie Wepner. Bawlie had allowed as to how Trixie Miggs had been a good-looking woman. Riley had observed that Bawlie seemed to be pretty well informed about the comings and goings at Trixie's house.

Bawlie Wepner had his problems, but he was not a bad-looking guy at all, not yet fifty. Mrs. Miggs had been thirty, attractive, unhusbanded, and living right next door. Nubs Tufo had called her a "hoor," but then he had the old-timer's regard for the fair sex. Five minutes at the Goose Step Inn on a busy night would probably be as much as Nubs could handle. Emil smiled to himself. It'd be as much as *I* could handle.

But *could* Bawlie Wepner be a suspect in the case?

Well, maybe, but not very likely. The chief suspect had to be the driver of the car Nubs Tufo had seen around four o'clock yesterday morning. Next came the owner of the green pickup and Felix "Flinch" Miggs, Trixie's husband. Maybe Corky had located Flinch by now. Lastly came the boy, Josh, but Emil had already dismissed the kid as a serious suspect. He'd acted strangely, been confused and run away, because he was simply scared to death.

Who wouldn't be?

"Ready to go, Emil?" Sarah asked, coming downstairs. "What do you know!" she cried, looking at him. "I can't get you to wear a tie for the life of me, but one mention of your name in the paper and—"

"What are you talking about?" he grumbled. "Got nothing to do with that."

During the drive to Crossroads, in spite of another brilliant, sunny day, Emil found his thoughts on the murder house. Was there something too obvious about that shattered clock? It all but waved its hands and said, "See me! See me! The time of the murders was 4:22."

Emil could not rid himself of the suspicion that, when everything seemed too clear, something important was missing.

Something had seemed missing, or not quite right, about Nubs Tufo too, and now Emil knew what it was: Nubs' dog, Stormy, the big Alaskan-Doberman half-breed. The door of Nubs' cabin had been ajar when he'd come down to the lake to hand over those license numbers. Surely Stormy would have come out with him, just as certainly as the dog would have accompanied Nubs on a run of his trap line.

Old dog, though. Very old. Could be sick, or might even have died, and in either case Nubs would not have mentioned it. Wasn't right to grieve for an animal, and it wasn't even good manners to grieve in public for a human being. Emil understood that way of looking at things, he was an old Stearns strong, silent type, but if Stormy had come to some disaster or demise, Nubs would be a little lonesome. Have to go out and drink some Tom and Jerries with him, Emil decided.

Stopped at a red light, Emil saw a glossy new Chrysler Imperial, gleaming black, coming up the street a whole lot faster than the law allowed, with the small, delicately engraved initials, WTB, on the front door, and saw the hunched bulk of Wilhelm Bundeswehr in the backseat. Emil also recognized red-haired but balding Father Rogers at the wheel. Bishop Bundeswehr made his chancellor do everything. It was a lesson in Christian humility.

"You could get a new coat, you know," Emil told Sarah as they drove on. "Present from me."

"No, no. If I have both a new coat and new dress at the Rosary Society investiture, it'll look like I'm showing off. Florence Hockapuk must feel badly enough as it is."

Florence wouldn't worry about you if she'd won, Emil thought.

Emil headed west on Division Street. There were a few morning skaters on little Lake George in the center of town, and some kids were setting up goals for a hockey game. In the summers, a pump and nozzle at the center of the lake shot a stream of water high into the air, one of the features of a city beautification project. Emil figured the water fountain was slightly superior to the scrawny cat on the Hannorhed bank's billboards. Division Street was all right in the residential district, but got into big trouble when it reached the west side, a chaos of supermarkets, automobile dealerships, and fast-food outlets. Thirty years earlier, there hadn't been much here except the baseball stadium—home of the St. Cloud "Rox"—and a little gray real estate shack. The shack was still here, but the stadium had been torn down, and as far as the eye could see were grotesque banners of neon calling attention to a disaster area. Some places had already gone out of business, standing blank-glassed and empty along the roadway, reproaching a disloyal and indifferent citizenry.

Emil pulled into the vast Crossroads shopping complex and dropped Sarah near the Dayton's entrance.

"I'm going over to the Auto Supply Center and get my new battery," he told her. "How about I meet you back here in an hour?"

"Oh, Emil, I can't buy a dress in just an hour!"

"Hour and a half."

"Two hours."

They settled on an hour and forty-five minutes, although Emil knew it would be two plus change.

"Well, howdy there, Emil," said Delbert Ebenscheider, chief of service at the Auto Supply, "come for your battery?"

"Can you install it right now?"

"You bet." Ebenscheider hollered for one of his boys to get on the job damn quick, make it yesterday, and invited Emil into his office for a cup of coffee from the machine. "Read about you in the paper this morning. Read about the whole thing. Pretty bad out at the Miggs house?"

"Yup."

"They find her husband yet? Flinch, the crazy bastard."

"I don't know."

"Thought Corky was relying on you all the way?"

"That was yesterday. No need to believe everything you read in the papers."

"Hell, I don't hardly believe none of it. You know, Flinch was in here night before last, long about two A.M."

"You don't say?"

"Yep. We pump gas twenty-four hours a day, you know, and now and then he'll take time off from making his rounds as Crossroads security guard to come over and have a cup of coffee. Only the other night he came over to get his pickup fueled to full. Nobody's seen him since."

"What kind of truck's he got?"

"Ford. Why?"

"Just curious. You called the sheriff's office with this information?"

"Nope. I'll tell Corky if he asks me, but otherwise I mind my own business. Flinch is mean. I don't want trouble."

"All right if I tell Corky when you saw Flinch Miggs?"

Delbert considered this. "If you don't say where you heard it. I don't want my name in the *Trib.*"

"Fair enough."

Emil and Delbert jawed awhile, solving world problems, while the new battery was installed. By the time Sarah climbed into the car with her glossy dress-box, the Russkies had been outfoxed, interest rates drastically reduced, the superiority of the older generation affirmed, and the Vikings victorious at the Super Bowl.

On the drive home, Sarah opened the box and showed Emil her new dress, a blue woolen knit.

"Looks nice," he said. That was what he always said.

"And I'm still a size ten," Sarah said proudly.

"Not bad for a woman your age."

Emil saw a Sheriff's Department car parked in front of his house when he swung into the driveway. Deputy Gosch was banging on the front door. He rushed down the steps and flapped a limp salute as Emil eased out of his car.

"Hello, Jamie," Sarah said. "Come in for a cup of coffee?"

"No can do, Missus Whippletree. Emil, can you go on over to the hospital right away? Corky's been trying to reach you ever since—well, he'll explain."

"Remember, we have to buy the tree today," Sarah whispered.

"Corky said I should drive you over to the hospital," Gosch bleated.

No point in refusing. Besides, Emil had to admit he was getting itchy to know how the case was going. He got in the patrol car, which Jamie piloted to the hospital, three blocks from Emil's house.

The sister on duty at the desk recognized Emil right away, and so did some of the folks in the lobby. Emil entered the elevator feeling pretty good. Maybe he shouldn't have retired after all.

Jamie led the old sheriff down a corridor to a room outside of which chunky Deputy Poll stood guard. Emil pushed open the wide hospital door and went inside. The room was crowded. Coroner Divot and Bureau of Criminal Apprehension officer Jiggsy Potoff stood near the window, which overlooked the Mississippi River. The white hospital bed held a thin pale boy with tangled blond hair and a tube in his arm. The boy was awake, but seemed only semi-alert. Corky Withers sat in a chair at the side of the bed, glaring at a man who stood, looking from the boy to Corky and back to the boy again, at the foot of the bed. The man turned when he heard Emil enter. He was lean, fairly tall, unshaven. Whether the expression on his face conveyed contempt or rude defiance was hard to tell. Scar tissue and a much-battered nose, narrow eyes, and a damaged mouth made nuances of feeling difficult to read. But the man grinned widely when he saw Emil, showing a gleaming row of false teeth.

"You must be Felix Miggs," Whippletree said.

"Call me Flinch, Emil." Flinch did not stand on formality. "I'm sure as hell glad you got here. Talk some sense into this—" He jerked his thumb in Corky's general direction.

Corky was on his feet. He looked tired, and about five years older than he had yesterday. But he wore a freshly pressed uniform and a profligate dose of lemon-lime aftershave.

"Emil, thanks for coming. The gist of the situation here is that—"

"Is that I don't want my boy answering questions, not a damn one!"

"You mean not until there's a lawyer present," suggested Emil. "Well, that's easy enough to—"

"No, I don't mean that. I mean no questions *at all,* you hear me?"

The boy listened to his raving father with a kind of dull-witted admiration.

"He don't have to say a single effing word," Flinch Miggs asserted, couching his language in genteel phraseology out of respect for his surroundings.

"But your son—ah, Josh might be able to give us some idea of who the killer is," Emil tried again.

Flinch twisted his face into an expression that might have approximated actual contempt, although it was hard to be sure.

"Don't give me that garbage," he said. "You're

just fishing. If you can't find anybody else to fit the bill, you'll nail the crime on my kid. I know how you boys operate."

Behind Flinch, Doc Divot was twirling a forefinger at his temple.

"I know how you operate, and me an' my boy are goin' to keep our mouths shut."

"Where were you at the time your wife and son were murdered?" Emil asked him.

"I ain't saying."

"Sheriff Withers, I'd advise you to arrest this man."

Corky looked surprised. Flinch looked astounded. "You can't do that! You ain't got a single—"

Emil took a few paces toward Miggs. Not that he could fight to any effect, but just to put a little authority in the statement. "We know," he told Flinch, "that you were absent from your job at the time of the murders. Corky, it's for real. Take him in for questioning."

Flinch Miggs seemed amazed. His assurance sagged momentarily, but long enough for Corky to get him in a hammerlock.

"You're under arrest for the murder of your wife and son!" Corky declared. "Poll! Gosch! Get in here!"

The deputies complied. Flinch was handcuffed. He struggled a little but not seriously, just a show for the sake of his reputation and vanity.

"Give him the cell in back," Corky instructed. "He shouldn't talk to anybody except a lawyer."

"Can't afford a lawyer, bastard," Flinch said.

"We'll fix you up with one. Get him out of here."

"Josh, don't say a goddam word about anything to any of these bastards," Flinch advised his son before Gosch and Poll took him away.

Josh watched his father's departure with bitter pride. He tightened his lips. His father's son. A toughie. Perhaps his mother's son too. What kind of woman would marry a man like Felix Miggs at—Emil calculated—the age of sixteen or seventeen? Flinch might have been less battered, but he couldn't have been much different, fourteen years ago.

"Nice goin', Emil," said Doc Divot. Jiggsy Potoff nodded in corroboration.

Corky drew Emil out into the corridor. "Where'd you come by that piece of news on Flinch?"

"Friend of mine out at the Crossroads told me."

"Emil, all hell has broken loose," Corky said with a perplexed, wounded look in those eyes Sarah had once said were "just like a young Paul Newman's."

"Well, tell me," Emil shrugged.

"I don't know if I should, unless—Emil, would you agree to be sworn in as a special deputy? Just for the duration of this case? I need your help and I've been getting a lot of flack for bringing you in yesterday without the proper procedures."

"Sure. Consider me sworn. Now what about this hell breaking loose?"

"Motor Vehicle called back on those license numbers, Emil. The truck belongs to a guy named Melvin Loftis. I've put out a bulletin on him. He's lead singer for that country band that plays at the Goose Step Inn."

"He'll be around," Emil said. "And the other number?"

Corky gulped. "The car is a Chrysler LeBaron, and it's registered to Father Peter Creedmore, out in Silverton."

The old sheriff thought it over. Country singer and country priest, both of them hanging around Trixie Miggs' house. But only Father Creedmore's car had been spotted there around the actual *time* of the murders.

"Oh, hell, I bet Father Peter's car was stolen that night, or something," Corky hoped.

"Better get Father rounded up for questioning PDQ."

"Well, I've called the Chancery already—" Corky faltered.

"The Chancery? Creedmore doesn't live at the Chancery. He lives in Silverton."

Corky looked at Emil as if he were, indeed, a little bit senile in his waning years. "Do you think I'm dumb enough to move on this without clearing it with Bishop Bundeswehr first? He is Father Creedmore's spiritual superior. He has to know. I'm waiting on a return call from the Chancery right now."

5

"The Miggs house is officially sealed according to BCA procedures," Jiggsy Potoff said. "Leander is typing up the final report over at our room in the Holiday Inn. But before he and I go back to The Cities, I want to cover some stuff with you."

Potoff and Emil, Corky and Doc Divot, all of them tense and a little somber, sat at a table in the hospital cafeteria's far corner.

"First," Jiggsy offered, "here is a picture of Mrs. Miggs. Before her head was blown away. The film was developed last month at the Loop Photomart, right here in St. Cloud. After finding the picture, I checked and learned it'd been taken by a friend of the deceased. On Thanksgiving night."

Thanksgiving as purveyed at the Goose Step Inn. No traditional scene around the groaning board, with old Tom Turkey brown and crisp, this colored snapshot showed Trixie dancing in costume. Looking straight into the camera. Smiling. Beaded headband. Feathers. Indian costume. Very brief Indian costume. Breasts visible almost to the nipples, slim legs flashing golden almost to the crotch. Behind her, in one corner of the picture, was the bandstand, on which a rangy long-haired young stud appeared to be sucking a microphone. His eyes were on Trixie, on her swaying body and bright flowing hair. She'd had a gorgeous body, soft, and a very pretty face, hard.

In the other corner of the picture, behind Trixie, Emil saw a section of the Goose Step's bar. Two men, seated on barstools, ogled Trixie as she danced.

One of them, in civilian clothes, was Courtney P. Withers, Jr. Seated next to him was Bawlie Wepner.

Emil looked at the photo, then passed it along to Corky, trying not to be too obvious as he watched the young sheriff's face.

"We found the picture in Mrs. Miggs' bureau drawer," Potoff informed everybody.

"Yes, I was there," Corky admitted, his face on fire. "But I didn't know her, I didn't know she was Mrs. Miggs. I swear I didn't. I didn't know Bawlie then, either." He looked at Emil, Potoff, and Divot in turn, meeting their eyes, but for no more than the shred of a second.

"Something like that, I'd look too," Potoff said. "Who wouldn't? All right, here are the photos that Leander took in the house."

"Hold on a second," said Emil. "Who was the friend that took this picture of Trixie Miggs?"

"Woman by the name of Ms. Tulip Mosey." Potoff emphasized the *Ms.* "Her camera and her film. I called her for personal verification after I'd checked with Photomart. She lives in Silverton. Very cooperative." Potoff turned to Corky. "Sheriff, she wonders why she hasn't been questioned yet, since she was Mrs. Miggs' best friend? Said anybody could find her almost any time out at this Goose Step Inn."

"We'll—we'll get to it in due course," Corky managed. "Tulip Mosey," he said, writing the name down on a piece of paper. "Don't know her either," he added unconvincingly.

Emil thought he saw a dubious squint in Potoff's left eye when the BCA investigator looked Corky's way, but then maybe Potoff was only recalling Corky's fear of Minneapolis television coverage.

"Now, this is how we found Mrs. Miggs' body," Potoff said, showing the picture.

Emil was incredulous. Father Creedmore had moved Trixie Miggs' body from its position in the chair and had lain it on the floor on top of all the buckshot. The crushed taco chips, in which there had been the trace of a footprint, were scattered all over. The beer bottles on the kitchen table had been arrayed in a neat row.

Corky had stood by and let the priest do these things, not protesting, not—apparently—saying a word.

Next, Potoff showed them a photograph of the bedroom in which Roger had come to doom. The boy had been moved from his deathbed onto the second mattress, taken from his own sleeping bag and placed on his brother Josh's, the better for Father Creedmore to anoint him.

"Do these pics reflect the way things looked when you entered the house?" Potoff asked. He had fallen into the pattern of directing his queries and remarks to Whippletree.

"I'll defer to Sheriff Withers on that question," Emil said drily.

Corky hesitated, faltered. But he was not the type of guy who could easily produce a lie, much less get it out without an impressive display of facial coloration. "No," he gulped. "Some things were moved."

Corky told Potoff what "things" had been moved.

"What?" cried the BCA agent. "Here Leander and me worked that house like specialists doing brain surgery, and everything was awry from the time we went inside! This is the . . ."

Whatever it was, Potoff decided against a detailed description. "Here are some pictures of the woman's bedroom," he said, with barely concealed exasperation. "What's been moved around in here?"

Corky looked at the pictures, shook his head. "Seems okay to me," he said. "Father Creedmore only went in there for a second. I don't know why."

Emil studied the photos. Bureau, closet, bed. Chair next to the bed, clothes on it. "Something's different in this one," he said.

"How's that?"

"When I went into this bedroom, a pair of panties lay on the floor next to the chair."

He showed them the picture and pointed to where the panties had been.

"You would notice something like that, wouldn't you, Emil?" cackled Doc Divot.

"Leander and me are straight as the day is long," glowered Potoff.

"*I* didn't take them or move them!" said Corky defensively.

The four men looked at one another.

"Well, it had to have been Father Creedmore," pronounced Doc Divot slowly.

Corky paled. The license number of that car . . .

"Now for fingerprints," said Potoff abruptly, "whatever the hell they're worth. Since it seems to me the crime site's been so irredeemably tainted that any defense lawyer worth his salt could get the whole ball of wax excluded as evidence, I offer these findings academically."

Father Creedmore's prints had been easy to identify. They had been found all over the house.

Doc Divot nudged Emil. "Looks like we got us another clergyman-killer here in Stearns County, eh?"

"Were Father Creedmore's fingerprints found anywhere in Mrs. Miggs' bedroom?" Emil asked.

Jiggsy Potoff consulted a long sheet of paper. "Only on a plastic statue of the Virgin. But those prints were old."

"You can tell?"

"Sure we can tell. Acid levels."

"Right."

"Other than family prints," Potoff continued, "which include those of Felix Miggs, her husband—"

"Also old prints?" asked Emil.

"Old and new. He's been there recently. Miggs has a record, you know. Six months in the St. Cloud Reformatory for passing bad checks. This was—let me see—seven years ago. Other than Mr. Miggs' marks, we found numerous unidentifiable prints belonging to two unknown individuals, for example on the light switch near the door."

"That would be me," Corky said guiltily. "I turned on the light without thinking."

Potoff made a check on his paper.

"I—I helped Father Creedmore," blithered Withers.

"I see."

"Well, he asked me to," Corky defended.

Potoff just shrugged. "The prints of the other unknown individual were found throughout the house," he said. "We also found a third set of prints, likewise unidentifiable at this time, on two weapons in the hall closet, a twelve-gauge shotgun and a thirty-aught-six rifle. Our computers are working on those now, but as you men know, if the prints aren't on file, they won't do us any good until we find the people to whom they belong."

"Any family prints on the two weapons?" Emil asked.

"Sure. All four of the family handled those weapons. Felix Miggs' prints, though, were very few and very old. Been a long time since he touched them. That's about all I have," Potoff concluded. "Doctor Divot?"

The coroner passed around copies of his autopsy reports on Trixie and Roger Miggs. "Not much to tell, but one thing I can say for sure, that broken clock on the wall is accurate. Death came at or about four A.M."

Emil pictured the road along Tufo's Lake, empty and eerie on a December morning, icy moon shining down. He saw the dark shadows of pine trees on the glowing snow, he was there beneath those pines, and a Chrysler LeBaron came up the road and turned into the Miggs' driveway.

A killer had come, living and breathing, out of the night and into that house. Emil felt the weird letter in his pocket. Should he mention it? Should he tell about the

phone call that threatened Sarah so vaguely? Potoff and
Fruth wanted to get back to the Twin Cities. Corky was
snowed under. Emil wasn't sure. I'll check a few things
out on my own, he thought.

A nun in a white habit came floating across the cafeteria. "Sheriff Withers," she said, "there's a phone call from
your office. It's urgent, they say. You may take it right over
there, at the phone behind the steam trays."

Corky got up and dog-trotted over to the phone. He
picked up the receiver, listened a minute, said something,
and hung up. When he came back to the table, Emil could
tell he was excited.

"Got some good news?" Doc Divot prodded.

"Sure hope so. Got to get back to the office right away.
Melvin Lotis, you know, the country singer, the one with
the GMC pickup? Well, he read Riley's story in the *Tribune* this morning, and he's over at my office now. He's
come forward for questioning."

6

Corky rushed from the hospital, forgetting that Emil had no transportation. After momentary irritation, Emil decided the hell with it. He shook hands with and said Merry Christmas to Divot and Potoff, then took an elevator back upstairs. He was a special deputy now, and he was more than a little curious to see if he could get any information out of Josh Miggs. Maybe he could make some headway with young Josh, in spite of Flinch's admonition that the boy "keep his mouth shut."

Emil really believed that there was no such thing as a bad kid.

When Emil stepped off the elevator, he saw Josh running up the corridor toward a fire exit. A Christmas tree, decorated to cheer visitors and patients, had been placed next to the elevator doors. Josh had to dodge it in order to reach the fire exit, no problem at all if Emil had not appeared. The boy saw Whippletree, but his mind was made up. He was getting out, bare ass and paper slippers and hospital gown. Emil braced against his cane, stuck out an arm, and felt the impact. He reeled, spun halfway around, but stayed on his feet. Josh Miggs bounced off Emil and careened into the wall next to the Christmas tree. Before he reached the door, Emil grabbed him by the upper arm.

"You gonna hit me?" the boy taunted, shivering in his skimpy gown.

"I'm doing you a favor, son. You'll never get out. Don't try it. The whole place is surrounded by cops, just to keep you in here. You're an important witness."

The part about the cops was untrue, but Emil figured it would impress the boy.

"Cops, huh?" said Josh, as if they were his due. "Let goa my arm, hey?"

"I will if you get back in your room. Otherwise we'll both be in big trouble."

Having a conspiracy seemed to please the kid, and he agreed to return to his bed. Emil got Josh into the room and back into bed, but the IV tube, which the boy had ripped from his arm, was making a puddle on the floor.

"What're you gonna do about that?" asked Josh.

"I'll make some excuse. Don't worry." The tube led to a bottle hanging upside down on a stand beside the bed. Emil turned off the flow of liquid.

"Say, who are you anyway?" the kid demanded, drawing a sheet over himself.

"Special deputy."

"Oh, yeah?"

"Yeah. I'm trying to find out who killed your mom and your brother."

"Get outta here," Josh said.

Emil didn't go.

"Thought I told you to get outta here."

"What happened in the house that night? What do you remember?"

"I'm not supposed to say nothin'."

"If you don't your dad will be in more trouble than he is already. He's got no alibi. The sheriff thinks he's the killer."

"It wasn't my dad!" sneered Josh. "That's stupid."

"Who was it?"

"I don't know."

"Did you see the person?"

"I—I think so. But I better not say nothin'."

"Son, I know what your dad said and I know how you feel, but it'd be better to tell what you remember as soon as possible. You might forget. And if you forget, it means whoever killed your mom and your brother will get off scot-free. Do you want that to happen?"

This made sense to Josh, but he was still doubtful. "You won't go tellin' my dad I squealed, will you?"

"I'd hardly call it squealing. But, no, I won't. It's a promise. We're working on this case together."

Josh liked that idea too. "But I don't remember much," he said.

"Just go ahead and tell me."

Then Emil and the boy were in the house on the murder night.

"I went to bed sort of late," Josh began. "Me an' Rog stayed up for Johnny Carson. Mom wasn't home yet when the show was over, so we went to bed."

"Where was your mother?"

"Out."

"Out where?"

"Out on a date!"

"You sound as if you weren't too happy about that. Who was she with?"

"That jerky singer from Silverton. She was always going out with him. Or he was always hanging around the house."

"Melvin Loftis?"

"That's the one. He drives a green truck."

"You didn't like him?"

"I can't stand him. He thinks he's going to be on a record some day. That's all he talks about. But he's not. He's not going to be on any record. He can't hardly sing."

That hasn't stopped a lot of them, Emil thought. "But your mom seemed to like this Loftis fellow, though?" he prodded.

"Yeah, I guess she did. She went out with him often enough."

"Do you remember when she came home?"

The boy shook his head, shivered. "I woke up real sudden, like I'd heard something, sort of an echo or something was in the house . . ."

First blast of the shotgun, Emil thought. Now Trixie is dead.

". . . I heard footsteps in the hallway. It was dark. I knew something was wrong. There wasn't time to do nothing. Somebody was in the doorway."

"You could see the person?"

"No, not then. I just—I just felt it."

"Did you say anything?"

"Just 'Rog.' I was going to wake him up. But then—" Josh faltered.

"Go ahead, son. I have to know. Just tell it fast and try not to think about it."

"Then the room flashed like a blue light and the explosion—I knew it was a gun then and I saw the man in the doorway. He'd shot Roger. It was like Roger and the mattress jumped up off the floor and fell back down. I didn't think of nothing but I rolled off my bed because somehow I knew—I knew he was there in the dark, swinging the gun toward me . . . and then there was the blue light and the explosion again and my mattress jumped off the floor—"

"Your sleeping bag was open. You weren't sleeping inside it?"

"It was too hot. I had my clothes on. I hadn't undressed."

"Why not?"

"Too much trouble. I was tired after the Carson show."

"And then what?"

"Then I was just lying there next to my mattress praying that he wouldn't turn on the light."

"You're sure it was a man? You couldn't have seen more than a silhouette, and not for more than a fleck of a second."

Josh thought about it. "It was somebody pretty big," he said. "I'm sure it wasn't no woman."

Somebody pretty big, Emil thought. Hardly a detailed description.

Now Trixie Miggs was dead in the kitchen, Roger dead in his sleeping bag—or bleeding to death there—and Josh huddled on the floor against the wall.

"Then what?"

"The footsteps went away. The gun exploded. It was so loud. I thought I'd go deaf. There was a click. Another explosion. Another click. And then the gun again."

Trixie has now been blasted into nothingness, Emil concluded. "And then you ran out of the house? Did you hear the killer leave?"

"No. I couldn't hear anything for a long time, because of the gunshots. I didn't hear anyone leave, and that scared me even more. So for a long time I just stayed there on the floor with my arms over my head, praying. Finally, I decided I had to get out, so I grabbed my shoes and a jacket from the closet by the door and ran outside."

"Did you look at your brother? Did you look in the kitchen?"

Josh shook his head. "I ran over to Mr. Tufo's cabin, but he wasn't there."

Nubs would already have been out checking his traps.

"Then I hid in Bawlie Wepner's truck."

"Hold it. You said you went to Tufo's cabin for help. So why didn't you pound on Bawlie's door, or something?"

"Because—because I thought it might have been *him*. The killer. I heard him and my mom yelling at each other once. They were real mad. She called him some names. Want to hear 'em?"

"No. That's all right. What were they arguing about?"

"Loftis. That stupid singer. Bawlie didn't want mom to go out with him, but she said she would go out with anybody she wanted to and he could go take a flying—"

"I get the picture. So you hid in the truck hoping to go to St. Cloud."

"Yeah, and find my dad at the shopping center."

"But then Bawlie found you and called the sheriff. Why'd you run away into the woods?"

So far, Josh's story had the ring of authenticity. If, however, he was telling the truth so far, his having fled into the woods made no sense.

"I—I started to think nobody would believe me," Josh confessed.

Emil honestly did not know whether to believe him or not. "Did Bawlie treat you badly at his place, after he found you in the truck?"

"No."

"Do you still think he might have been the person with the shotgun?"

"He could of been covering up by being nice to me," the kid offered.

"Maybe it was your dad in the house?"

Josh looked offended. "The only person he might kill would be Melvin Loftis."

"He's said this?"

"That's what he told mom. He didn't like her seeing Loftis *at all.*"

"Did Loftis and your mother ever quarrel?" Emil asked. "That you know of?"

"Sometimes."

"About what?"

"Like he has this other girl. Two-lips, or something."

Tulip Mosey, Emil remembered. The girl who'd taken the photograph of Trixie Miggs on Thanksgiving.

"Mom didn't like that."

"Maybe Melvin Loftis came to your house with a gun?" Emil suggested.

Josh shook his head. "Naw. He's too skinny. The guy in the doorway was bigger."

Flinch Miggs was wiry of build, Whippletree reflected. But two suspects were not. Bawlie Wepner. And Father Peter Creedmore.

Yet he could not make surmises on the sole basis of Josh Miggs' minisecond glimpse of the killer.

"You've been a big help—" he was telling the boy, when a nurse entered the room, trailed by Deputy Axel Vogel.

"Emil, here you are!" Axel exclaimed happily. "Corky said to come and pick you up."

"What happened to the IV tube?" asked the nurse, eyeing Josh accusingly.

Emil came through for the kid, just as he had promised.

"My fault," he said apologetically. "Got the crook of my cane twisted up in it. It was really stupid of me. I was just going to come and get you."

The nurse's expression revealed a less than flattering estimation of Emil's IQ.

"Really sorry," he said to her.

"You ought to be." She prepared to reinsert the device.

"He ain't nothing but a clumsy old duffer," Josh Miggs said, grinning meanly.

So much for good kids.

7

Axel Vogel was a heavyweight in the basic sense of the word.

"Had breakfast yet, Emil?" he inquired, while driving the old sheriff from hospital to home.

"Three hours ago."

"How about lunch? They got a good plate of pig's knuckles and knoedel at the Courthouse Bar and Grill."

"Sorry. Got to get home today. Sarah wants to go shopping for a tree."

"Yeah, sure," Axel said.

Emil wouldn't have minded a big roast beef sandwich, but his knee had begun to throb again, and he wanted to get home and take one of those pills Doc had prescribed.

Corky changed the format.

"Emil, can you get over to the jail?" he asked, his voice an electric snarl over the two-way.

"Sure thing. Got to stop off at home for a minute though."

He was glad he did. Sarah looked puzzled.

"Emil, we had the strangest phone call. You won't believe it."

"What?" He got a pill out of the medicine chest in the downstairs bathroom and gulped it down without water.

"It was a man," Sarah said. "Good Lord, drink some water. At least I think it was a man. Do you know what he said?"

"No," said Emil, staying calm. He braced himself.

"He said something so strange: 'If you harm the helpless, then the helpless will be harmed.' Isn't that odd? It gave me the shivers."

Emil thought it over. Either a nutso or somebody who knew exactly what he was doing. Emil suspected the latter.

"Probably a nutso," he told Sarah. "Don't worry about it at all. Keep all the doors and windows locked."

"Oh, you," said Sarah, paling slightly. "I will," she added.

Then Axel drove Whippletree downtown, where Flinch Miggs was screaming at the end of the cellblock. His voice carried into Corky's office.

"I'm innocent!" he howled. "Bring on the lie detector! What do you think I am, anyway? Some kind of second-class citizen? Hitch me up to a lie detector. *Now!*"

He paused to acknowledge the enthusiastic applause of the current guests of Stearns County: habitual drunk Fred Stroheim, would-be con man Bob Meyer, failed liquor store holdup specialist Reuben Resinger, and Myrtle "Dolly" Ludenbach, who signed the register as "professional masseuse."

When the accolades subsided, Flinch started yelling again.

"Loftis? I know you're out there, Loftis! Come back here! Hey, you ain't got the guts to come back here! But come back here and give me your best shot, and then we'll see what happens!"

The inmates cheered again. "Yeah, Loftis. Come back and sing us a song," urged Dolly Ludenbach.

Melvin Loftis looked pained. Where was it written that the lead singer of The Long Prairie Boys should have to sit in the sheriff's office, hard by the jail? Bad enough to be suspected of murder. Even worse to put up with humiliating taunts, although it was sort of flattering that Dolly had asked him to sing.

"Emil, this here's Melvin Loftis," Corky said. "As soon

as he read Riley's story in the *Trib* this morning, he decided to come in on his own volition and help us out with the case. Loftis, you know Sheriff Whippletree? He's special deputy on this case, or will be as soon as we find a Bible and swear."

"'Course I know Emil." Loftis grinned, offering his hand.

Emil shook hands. He had never met Loftis before. The guy had a limp shake, in spite of the guitar calluses on his fingers.

"Loftis, come on back here and take your best shot!" Flinch Miggs howled again. "Come on, if you're man enough."

"Alyce, close the door to the cellblock," Corky directed his secretary.

The country singer wore a pained look, two-toned cowboy boots, tight old blue jeans that pushed outward his clump of genitalia, and a beige suede jacket with fake rawhide fringe. He had on a black T-shirt under the jacket, which hung partially open, so that Emil was afforded a glimpse of the wisdom there:

I'LL GET ON
MY KNEES
IF YOU GET ON
YOUR ELBOWS

Loftis had a long, indolent body. Maybe he was strong, maybe he wasn't. You couldn't tell. He had thick, dark blow-dried hair. Smooth face, pouty mouth, arrogant eyes. Melvin smiled a lot, probably to distract people from his eyes. He would be real nice and phony to a woman, Emil understood, until he got her interested in him. Then he would change overnight and be a real bastard, which the kind of woman he attracted had probably wanted all along.

He decided that he wouldn't trust Melvin Loftis as far as the court house, and that was just across the street.

Sheriff Corky Withers, however, was of another mind.

"Melvin here," he told Emil, "says he wants to give us some information. I'd like you to sit in on this, Emil, if you don't mind."

"Be glad to."

Loftis smiled, but his eyes betrayed a certain lack of enthusiasm for the old sheriff's presence. Con jobs always work better one-on-one.

"Go ahead, Melvin."

Loftis smiled and ducked his head self-effacingly. "Well, it's this way. I read the story in the newspaper this morning, and I just couldn't believe it. Trixie! She and I were..." He supplied a loose gesture to indicate how they had been. "We were real good friends. I can't believe she's dead. And then I saw the license number of my truck, right there in the *Trib*. You can imagine how upset I was. Who turned in the license number, by the way?" he asked offhandedly.

Before Emil could make a sign or head him off, Corky spilled the beans. "Norbert Tufo," he said proudly.

Melvin's face darkened.

"Understand you tried to dump some garbage on Tufo's property?" Emil drawled. "He let you off easy. Nubs and I are from the old school. Something belongs to us, we take it seriously."

The singer glanced at Emil, reappraising him. Melvin's tone was considerably more guarded when he spoke again.

"Anyway," he said, "I want you to know that I'll cooperate in any way I can."

"Where were you on the night of the murders?" Emil asked.

Either Melvin was telling the truth or he had rehearsed astutely. "Till two I was at the Goose Step Inn. Doing my gig with the guys until midnight or so, then having a few and unwinding."

"After that?"

"I spent the night with"—feigned coyness—"a young lady. At her place."

"Name of said young lady?"

"Well, I—ah—don't like to say."

"I understand how you feel—" Corky began.

"How'd you like to be booked on suspicion, back there in a cell next to Felix Miggs?" Emil asked.

"I was with a woman named Tulip Mosey," Loftis answered hastily. "She hangs out at the Goose Step."

"Friend of Mrs. Miggs, wasn't she?" demanded Emil.

Corky looked at his predecessor, puzzled. "Emil, where did you get this information?"

Emil waved him off.

"Look, Loftis, two people are dead, and I don't like it. Don't get cute. I know you spent time in the Miggs house, and I figure a hell of a lot of fingerprints there belong to you. Corky, make a note to get this guy printed, send them down to the BCA in The Cities."

"Sure I visited Trixie," Loftis admitted, lifting his hands, palms outward.

"You did more than visit her, didn't you? And now you're spending your nights with this Mosey woman. So, as I asked a moment ago, were Mosey and Mrs. Miggs friends?"

"It went on and off," Loftis said.

"Just like you did, right? First with one and then with the other. But you have an alibi, isn't that convenient?"

Loftis turned sullen. "I'm not sayin' anymore if this is the way you're gonna treat me."

Corky seemed agitated, as if a nice social situation had just been scotched by a rude guest.

"You don't have to say much more right now," Emil told him. "I know plenty about you. That you tried to dump garbage on property belonging to a friend of mine. That you were one of Trixie Miggs' lovers. That you quarreled with her over Ms. Mosey. And that Flinch Miggs wanted to kill you."

Loftis paled a shade or two.

"Didn't know that, did you?"

"But Flinch and Trixie were separated."

"Apparently she thought they were more separated than he did. Corky, do you have any more questions for Mr. Loftis?" Emil asked.

"Ah . . . no. Melvin, go out there in the front office and have Deputy Poll fingerprint you, if it's no trouble."

Loftis grunted, whether in acquiescence or resignation was hard to tell, muttered a "see ya," and walked out.

"Where did you find out that stuff?" Corky asked.

"I talked to Josh Miggs for a little while."

"Think he's telling the truth?"

"Maybe."

"It's pretty much immaterial now, though," Corky said.

"It is?"

"Right. First off, if Melvin's fingerprints match the ones we found around the house, that takes care of that. One set is me, the other is him."

"What about the prints on those two guns in the closet? Those are the only ones not accounted for."

"So what? Irrelevant. Those guns weren't used in the murders. A different gun was used. A double-barreled shotgun, ten-gauge. And we've got it!"

"We have?"

"Flinch's pickup was parked in the hospital lot. Jamie Gosch checked it out. Found the shotgun and two and a half boxes of shells under the seat. Weapon's been fired *very* recently, too."

"What does Miggs say?"

"Says he bought it for himself as a Christmas present, took it out, and fired it for target practice day before yesterday."

"Where did he say he was on the night of the killings? When he was absent from his job?"

"Said he was driving around looking for Melvin Loftis, to beat the living shit out of him. I think his alibi's a bunch of garbage. Flinch Miggs is a wild man. He's the killer, all right. The court's getting him a lawyer and we'll give him that polygraph test if he wants it. But, hell, Emil, it's all plain as the nose on your face. Flinch Miggs is our man."

"Wait just a minute here, Corky. What about Father Creedmore? His car was at the *scene* of the crime at the *time* of the crime. What about that?"

Young Sheriff Withers smiled. "Father Creedmore is waiting for one of us to call on him. He'll explain everything. Father Rogers, from the Chancery, called to report that Bishop Bundeswehr has worked everything out."

"Creedmore is waitin for one of *us* to call on *him?*" asked Emil.

"Sure," said Corky. He was pretty relaxed now, with the case all wrapped up. "Emil, I'll be tied up with Flinch and everything. How about if I have one of the boys drive you out to Silverton to register Creedmore's statement? Shouldn't take very long."

Emil glanced at his watch. Lunchtime. Well, what the hell, grab a sandwich somewhere, go on out to Silverton and satisfy my curiosity. More than curiosity. He was convinced that Flinch Miggs—in spite of his anemic alibi—hadn't killed anybody. In point of fact, Emil's major suspicions were tending toward Melvin Loftis, and Bawlie Wepner's role niggled somewhere at the back of his mind too.

Nor could he any longer dismiss Josh Miggs as the possible killer. Thinking back on the scene in the hospital room, recalling the boy's mood and tone, Emil faced the fact that he might have been hornswoggled by a clever liar.

"Got to use your phone and tell Sarah where I'll be," he

told Corky. "Today was our day to buy a Christmas tree, but there ought to be plenty of time for that. Say, Corky," he added. "Think you could have Alyce give Sarah a ring every now and then? Just until I get back from Silverton?"

"Sure," Corky said.

8

Roy Riley's black Dodge van was parked at the side of the jail when Emil went outside. The reporter was fiddling with a strange-looking antenna protruding from the roof of the vehicle. "What's been happening in Stearns County law enforcement lately?" Riley grinned.

"Why don't you go inside and ask?"

"Can't. I'm barred. Sheriff Withers has 'declined comment,' as we say in the trade. He didn't like my story this morning. He has also forbidden me access to his office, unless I get arrested, I suppose."

Riley seemed in good cheer, though. He jiggled the bizarre contraption a bit, stuck his head inside the van, withdrew, and then adjusted the device with a light, final touch.

"What the hell is that thing?" Emil asked. He looked toward the parking lot, where Axel Vogel was warming up one of the Stearns County cars for the trip to Silverton.

"With this little piece of wire . . ." Riley began. "No, you wouldn't be interested."

"You could try me."

"I heard a rumor to the effect that you've been made a special deputy on this case. That true?"

"I guess it is."

"Come on, Emil. I know Flinch Miggs is in there, under arrest on suspicion. I know the license plates belong to Melvin Loftis, who just came out, and to Father Peter Creedmore of Silverton."

"How did you—?"

"Anyone with a telephone can dial the motor vehicle office in The Cities. What's Father Creedmore's connection to this case?"

Axel Vogel came to Emil's rescue. Stearns County Car Number Three pulled to the curb. Emil opened the door and slid inside.

"Where you headed, Sheriff?" Riley tried.

"Home," said Emil. By a roundabout route, he qualified to himself.

In the car, Whippletree remembered something: the package of Salem cigarettes on Trixie Miggs' kitchen table. Roy Riley also smoked Salems. "You go out carousing much at night?" he asked Axel.

"Now and then. Knock back a few, is all. Why?"

"Ever see Riley around at night?"

"Nope. Can't say as I have. Usually he has his lunch at the Courthouse Bar and Grill. Picks up the gossip, I guess."

Emil put the reporter out of his mind, reached for his pack of Red Man, and put a hefty pinch between cheek and gum.

"Glad I'm driving you," Axel said. "It was getting pretty antsy back in the office."

"Why's that?"

"Well, first there was arresting Flinch. Then the St. Paul *Pioneer Press* gives Corky a phone call. About the murders."

"What did he tell them?"

"He didn't tell them nothing. He had Alyce tell them he was out. And after that there was a call from Father Rogers, over at the Chancery."

"What did he want?"

"I don't know, but whatever it was upset old Corky. He was standing there by the phone like he was at attention or something and saying, 'Yes, Father, no, Father, Yes, Father' like he was a little kid caught with his hand in the poor box."

Axel was famished, as always, and Emil was a little hungry, so they stopped for a minute at the Dippi-Freez on Division Street. Whippletree ordered bratwurst with sauerkraut, hard roll, and coffee. Axel opted for the Christmas Special, a monstrous hot fudge sundae in a plastic dish shaped like Santa's sleigh.

Dink Kufelski, the owner of Dippi-Freeze, came over to ask if everything was all right and how the murder investigation was coming along.

"Everybody thinks you did it, Dink," Axel told him.

The drive to Silverton after lunch was pleasant and short. Axel full was Axel content and quiet. Whippletree looked out over the land he loved like a brother and knew like the back of his hand. The sky was clear, but way off to the northwest, just along the horizon, a thin gray haze was forming.

"Snowstorm or blizzard by tomorrow night," he said to Axel.

"Naaaaw," said the deputy disbelievingly. "Can't have a blizzard now. It'd fuck up Christmas. God wouldn't allow nothing like that."

"Hope you're right." A snowstorm was just about the last thing Emil wanted. If the storm happened to be bad, the roads from Iowa would be impassable, and he wouldn't get to see Hugh. Emil had begun to realize that he had maybe one, maybe ten, maybe only a few more times to see his brother in his life. It was true, as Sarah always observed, that the two of them never said much and "sat there like bumps on a log." But just sitting there with Hugh, reading, watching TV, whatever, put Emil back in touch with his boyhood, his roots, his life.

Silverton was quiet when they arrived, Main Street cold and vacant at lunchtime. Windblown snow, fine as powder, drifted against the tires of parked cars. Two pickup trucks, a battered Mercury, and a big International Harvester tractor with an enclosed cab were parked in front of the Goose Step Inn. A handpainted wooden sign hanging next to the door heralded MELVIN LOFTIS AND THE LONG PRAIRIE BOYS!

Axel parked the patrol car in the rectory's driveway, next to the church. The rectory was set back from the street behind a scraggly row of dying cypress, to which inadequate garlands of Christmas tree lights had been attached. There was a car already in the drive, a blue Lincoln. Father Creedmore's Chrysler LeBaron was probably in the garage next to the house.

"Lincoln, hey," said Axel. "Hot stuff." He switched off the ignition. "I'd kind of like to trot across to the Goose Step there and have me some fried fatback and mashed potatoes."

"Go ahead," Emil told him. "When I'm through with Father Creedmore, I'll come on over and buy you a beer. Just keep your eye out, though, in case whoever owns this Lincoln wants to leave. You'll have to move our car."

"Sure thing."

Axel waddled toward the Goose Step Inn. Emil made his way up the rectory's flagstone walk and rang the doorbell.

"Yes?" said a chubby old lady in an ancient housecoat. Her smile was of the vague variety, and Emil had the feeling that this woman wasn't all there.

"I'm Emil Whippletree. From the sheriff's office. Here to see Father."

She gave him her vacant smile.

"I'm expected," he said.

"Who is it, Mother?" called a voice from the next room, and then Father Creedmore strode from the room toward Emil.

"Sheriff, come in, come in! I've been waiting for you."

He put his hands on the woman's shoulders, drawing her away from the door so that Emil could enter. "You did just fine, Mother," he told her. "Now, why don't you go back to the ironing? The *ironing*," he repeated, and the woman returned, apparently, to her chore.

"Mother is my housekeeper," Father Creedmore told Emil, leading him back into the sparsely furnished house. "It spares me a lot of vicious talk, as you can imagine."

Emil reached out, took in and salted away his impressions of Father Peter Creedmore. The physical man who had brought last rites to the Miggs house was here before him: powerful shoulders, thick body, yet the priest moved lightly on his feet. In good shape. Undistinguished face save for hard black eyes and a faintly unpleasant expression, as if some obscure, perpetual pain befouled his private dreams.

Whippletree felt a chill of recognition. He had been around long enough to know what he liked and what he didn't. And he had experienced this form of instant antipathy before, this suspicious, jittery wariness, upon meeting the murdering minister, Matthew Koster.

"Come on in, Sheriff, and have a seat," Creedmore said, motioning Emil toward a chair. "Do you still use the title?"

"I don't. Some do. If they want to, fine with me. Sheriff's the only title I ever had."

"Oh, no, 'mister' is also a title," the priest corrected.

"It's the only one he has now."

The voice had sounded different over the phone, no less supercilious perhaps, but more insidious, as if its proprietor preferred to strike from a distance.

"Oh, I'm so sorry," exclaimed Father Creedmore. "Mr. Whippletree, I'd like you to meet Eugenio Spritzer, lay director of the Life Saviors."

Eugenio was extraordinarily short, and he did not rise to shake hands. Emil wondered what he was doing here. Father Creedmore produced a hanger and Emil hung up his coat.

The room into which Emil had been taken was Father Creedmore's office-study. Chilly and rather dark, it was on the north side of the stone house. Where bookshelves did not line the walls, there were posters of various sizes showing fetuses at different stages of development. Each poster screamed, in large red letters, STOP THE DEATH MERCHANTS. A thick stack of similar posters rested on Creedmore's desk.

No one spoke for a moment. The priest sat down behind his desk. He was smiling. He seemed at ease. On his wrist, alongside a big watch, was the rubber band Emil had seen him wearing at the Miggs house.

"Well," said Creedmore expansively, "go ahead."

Emil glanced in Spritzer's direction. He had no intention of discussing a murder case in the presence of a staring stranger.

"Eugenio's a friend of mine," Creedmore hastened to explain. "He knows all about it."

"That's right," affirmed Spritzer, with a combination of fear, rancor, and aggression, "I know all about it."

Whippletree, who had expected a man-to-man talk, realized that Eugenio Spritzer was here as a witness. He turned to look the little guy square in the face. Spritzer, flushing slightly, met Emil's eyes and lifted a pointy chin.

"Whereabouts in the county you from?" Emil asked Spritzer. He had a feeling that he was being set up here, maneuvered into a situation not intended to do him any good.

"Holdingford," Spritzer said, with dislike for Emil in his eyes and voice.

"Holdingford, sure," drawled Emil. Yes, he had known a tribe of Spritzers out Holdingford way in years past. He was also able to determine Spritzer's age. More than a dozen Stearns County babies had been baptized "Eugenio" in 1939. There'd been a new Pope that year.

"You've been gone from the county for a bit?" Whippletree asked Spritzer. "I think I recollect your people, but still can't place you personally."

Spritzer fidgeted. "I was—"

"Eugenio studied for the priesthood at Pater Noster,"

Father Creedmore explained, mentioning the big abbey north of St. Cloud. "But he left it to serve Christ as a layman at St. Concepta's in Big Falls."

Whippletree nodded. If this were true, he gave old Spritzer credit. St. Concepta's, better known as "the home," was a mental institution. Working there was no picnic.

"Father was chaplain there for a time," Eugenio added. "That's where we became friends and decided our interests were similar. I was sorry to give up my work at the home, but Life Saviors needs dedicated souls, as do all our godly endeavors."

"I understand Mrs. Whippletree may be named next head of the Rosary Society," said Father Creedmore.

"She has been. She's been elected."

"It's an important job. We need the best people in positions like that," Spritzer said.

"Well, Sheriff," said the priest, "let's get down to business and do what's expected of us."

This is my chance to find out what's going on, thought Emil. He noted that Eugenio Spritzer had slipped a hand into the pocket of his suitcoat. Spritzer's hand was small, but somehow it filled that pocket.

"You sure you've got your tape threaded right?" he asked the little man.

Spritzer flushed as red as a county fair blue-ribbon Royal Ruby beet.

"Eugenio, I'm surprised at you," scolded Father Creedmore sadly. "Why don't you just go chat with mother until Sheriff Whippletree and I are through?"

Spritzer slunk out of the room, glowering. He didn't look at Emil.

"I'm sorry, Sheriff. He's just very devoted to me. I hope you don't get the wrong idea."

"Peculiar guy, isn't he?" Emil observed. "You sure he was on the *staff* up at St. Concepta's in Big Falls?"

A look of pain crossed Father Creedmore's broad face, a sharper pain than the one he seemed constantly to bear.

"Why'd you move the bodies in that house?" Emil demanded, getting down to brass tacks. "Why'd you deliberately get your fingerprints all over the evidence?"

Father Creedmore had not expected an assault. He leaned back slightly in his big leather chair, blinked, and laced his fingers before him.

Emil had always believed, perhaps prejudicially, that people who steepled their fingers were conceited, and that people who laced their fingers were trying to figure out a plausible lie.

"It was agreed that I am to read you a statement, Mr. Whippletree."

"Fine, Father. Read it."

Creedmore looked put-upon, irritated. "I mean, I didn't realize—what I mean is that I didn't expect questions. That was the agreement."

"All I know is that Corky sent me out here for facts we need in the case. I don't know anything about an agreement."

Father Creedmore's eyes showed anger, a sudden, searing rage. Muscles rippled along his thick jawline. He took the rubber band from his wrist and began to fiddle with it. "The agreement," he said, speaking very softly, looking directly at Whippletree's mouth, "was between Sheriff Withers and the Chancery. I am to make a statement, if you would be so kind as to copy it down? That is what His Excellency arranged."

Corky didn't even have the guts to tell me, Emil thought, getting more suspicious by the moment. He had the feeling of being set up again, gulled into treacherous territory.

"All right, read me your statement."

Relaxing perceptibly, Creedmore slipped the rubber band back on his wrist and pulled a folded piece of paper from beneath a stack of fetus posters. He unfolded it ceremoniously and cleared his throat.

"You write it yourself?" Whippletree asked lazily, twirling his pencil.

"Yes!"

"Just asking."

Creedmore began to read. "Early on the morning of the murders, I had occasion to leave my rectory for the purpose of calling upon Mr. Mott Heiderscheidt, of rural Silverton, who is a member of my parish suffering a terminal illness."

"At that time, Father?" Emil asked. "Middle of the night?"

"I couldn't sleep," said the priest. "I just had a feeling. I'd been out to visit them earlier that day, and Mott seemed to be sinking."

Emil nodded. Could have happened. "Go on."

"On the drive to the Heiderscheidt residence, however, I made a wrong turn down one of the many country lanes that abound in Stearns County. Realizing my error, I turned around in the driveway of the Miggs' property, at which time the number of my license plate was apparently noted by Mr. Norbert J. Tufo."

"When you turned around," Emil asked, "did you know it was the Miggs' driveway?"

Creedmore's story was plausible so far. The Heiderscheidts lived down a road not far away from Tufo's Lake.

"Yes, I *knew* it was the Miggs' driveway," Creedmore answered, exasperated. "I *know* the people of my parish."

Emil shrugged. "Sorry."

"Where was I?" asked the priest, finding his place. "Oh, yes. . . . Correcting my error, I turned around, drove to the Heiderscheidt farmhouse, where I administered the sacrament of Extreme Unction. I then drove directly home."

"Mott's still hanging on, though, isn't he?"

"Yes, he is, thank God," said the priest, looking up. "May I continue?"

"Fine with me."

"On the next day, just before noon, I received a call from Stearns County Sheriff, Courtney P. Withers, Jr., informing me that Mrs. Trixie Miggs and her son, Roger, had been killed, and that last rites were in order. And so it was that I entered the house to administer the sacrament there."

Creedmore stopped reading. "That's all I have," he said.

"That's all?"

Creedmore slipped the rubber band off his wrist again, and began pulling and tugging at it. "What else is there to say? That's what happened."

"Well, there are a few questions that come to mind."

"*Mr.* Whippletree, apparently you have not been informed as to the manner in which this investigation is being conducted, or you cannot *remember* the arrangement reached between His Excellency and the sheriff, but—"

"Why'd you move the bodies in that house?" Emil asked, as he had earlier. "Why'd you go and get your fingerprints all over the place?"

Creedmore stretched the rubber band and strummed it hard, producing the sound of a sick guitar string. "I have nothing to hide," he said, "everybody knows that."

"So, what about inside the house? Why'd you move things around?"

"Because Sheriff Withers assured me it was all right to do so! I assumed the investigation, the—whatever has to be done—was *done*. I wanted to anoint the bodies as correctly as possible. You know there was little I could do in the case of Mrs. Miggs"—he played a mad riff on the rubber band—"but that, I suppose, was God's will. I never *imagined* I was doing anything wrong."

"Corky didn't stop you? From moving the bodies, or taking the boy from his sleeping bag?"

Creedmore lifted his hand. "As God is my witness. And, although questions were not to have been permitted, you may record my answers."

"Thanks. Corky said, by the way, that you were the one who gave orders inside the house?"

"Sheriff Withers is mistaken."

"Your fingerprints were found on a plastic statue of the Virgin, on Trixie Miggs' dresser."

Creedmore slipped the rubber band back onto his wrist, next to the watch. "Every family in my parish received such a figurine, personally blessed by me, on the Feast of the Assumption," he said.

"All right. But tell me one thing, Father. Would you be willing to take a lie detector test? Naturally, you'd want to consult an attorney of your choice first."

Father Creedmore's face darkened, veins at his temples pulsated in spasms.

"I have nothing to hide," he said, rising. "You insult me. You insult the Holy Mother Church."

"I didn't say anything about any church."

"I feel our interview is at an end."

"Suits me. Didn't mean to get you so riled, Father."

"I am *not* riled. I am—"

Whippletree got up from his chair and grabbed his coat off the hanger.

"I am . . . *appalled,*" Creedmore clarified. "A man like you, who knows how things are run in the county, who has lived here a lifetime—"

"Don't assume that we're all the same," Emil replied, with a flash of anger. Like most folks in Stearns County, he'd been born into a family that took its practice of religion seriously. But God had saddled him with a skeptical temperament: he didn't figure you had to trust people automatically just because they made a living by telling the faithful to believe in things that couldn't be seen. Emil's own churchgoing was mostly for the purpose of making Sarah happy. A good enough reason, he thought.

Indulging a sudden suspicion, Emil stepped quickly to the door and pulled it open.

"Oh!" exclaimed a startled Eugenio Spritzer, "I was just—"

"I'm leaving," Emil told him. He walked to the front door, conscious of furious Creedmore behind him, and of Spritzer bringing up the rear.

"Corky thinks Flinch Miggs is the culprit," Emil said, turning at the door.

Creedmore's face was still dark from the angry blood beneath his skin. Even the whites of his eyes were discolored. "It's possible," he said. "Those Miggs are not—" He seemed to catch himself.

"Are not what?" Whippletree pumped.

"—are not like you and me," the priest finished.

"I'm not that good on distinctions," Emil said. Then he hit Father Creedmore with his last question. "What about the panties, Father?" he asked.

Eugenio Spritzer paled, but the priest's anger faded quickly into stark bewilderment.

"Mr. Whippletree, what in God's name are you talking about now?" he cried.

Emil, however, was not so easily thrown off the track. "I'm afraid that's my man," he murmured, limping down the rectory steps, making his way toward the Goose Step Inn. Father Creedmore had shown obvious signs of great stress, while the little he had revealed was couched in dry phrases—*Realizing my error, I turned around in the driveway*—or colored by what Emil deduced to be a tendency toward rage.

Two additional points also seemed telling: Not once had Father Creedmore spoken of Trixie Miggs or her son in reflective, human terms, the way good-hearted people, and especially the clergy, generally mention those who have died. And, secondly, Father Creedmore's only companion in the rectory was his aging mother, who was probably incapable of registering his arrivals and departures, let alone remembering them.

Trouble was, what could the motive have been? Whippletree, way out there in the heady ranges of square ninety-nine, close to home, had to turn around, had to hunch and tilt his way back to square one.

"Mr. Whippletree! Mr. Whippletree!"

Emil turned. Eugenio Spritzer came out of the rectory and hurried after him.

"Well, Spritzer," Emil said, "it's been a pleasure meeting a fellow as interesting as yourself. Sarah and I've enjoyed your phone calls too."

"What on *earth* are you talking about now?"

"You've got a distinctive voice, Eugenio. Get somebody else to make harassing calls for you. Question is, what the hell are you doing it for?"

"I am *not* doing it," said Spritzer.

He was one of those ballsy little Napoleonic types. Emil had half an impulse to believe him. Then he remembered the tape recorder that Spritzer had concealed in his pocket.

"Fellow who would go bugging people doesn't strike me as too reliable," he said.

"Father didn't know anything about that!" Spritzer crossed his arms and stared at Emil challengingly.

"Oh, sure," said Emil.

"I mean, it was my idea to tape the conversation. Naturally, I didn't, not after Father voiced his displeasure."

"Not after I spotted what you were up to."

"And it's my idea to talk to you now. Father knows nothing about it. He's retired to his study, deeply depressed. Mr. Whippletree, you did that to him, and our people simply cannot have Father depressed!"

"Your people?"

"The Life Saviors. We rely on Father Creedmore to lead us against the merchants of death. Mr. Whippletree, we won't allow anyone to stir up a hornet's nest around Father Peter Creedmore. Not *anyone.*"

"You know any reason why Father Pete might have wanted to kill Trixie Miggs?" he asked. He expected Spritzer to get all mad, jump up and down a little. But the diminutive lay director of Stearns County Life Saviors surprised him.

"Sheriff, I can think of reasons why a lot of people might have wanted to kill her, and I can think of at least one reason why it might have crossed Father's mind as well. But he did *not* do it! You have to understand that immediately and *get off his back!*"

"I'd hardly say I was on his back when he has Bishop Bundeswehr running interference for him."

"No, Sheriff, you are driving him off the deep end with your suspicion, and he is a harmless, helpless—"

Spritzer's eyes widened slightly as if he'd said something he hadn't intended. Emil recalled what the anonymous messenger had said to Sarah: *If you harm the helpless, then the helpless will be harmed.* Was that simply the lunatic riddle of a feverish brain, or did it actually mean something? And if it did, who was harmless and helpless?

Spritzer obviously thought Father Creedmore was.

"I've seen Father's shoulders and arms," Emil drawled. "Hardly the pushover type, I'd say. Does seem pretty nervous to me, though. You're right about that. But maybe he's got good reason. And that," Whippletree leaned forward and poked Spritzer smartly in the chest, "is what I aim to find out."

"Oh, you do, do you?"

"Yeah. You can bet your ass on it."

"Don't be crude, Mr. Whippletree."

"I adjust to fit the company."

Spritzer reddened. "You're so pathetic, really. You understand nothing. Father may be afraid of you, but I'm not."

"You call me on the phone again without saying your name and you *will* be afraid, believe me," Emil shot back. Getting mad, he realized. Calm down.

"I've said my last word on the subject," Spritzer declared, turning away, and retreating back inside the rectory.

Emil went on over to the Goose Step Inn, figuring that if Peter Creedmore was afraid of him, his investigation was on the right track. But he was only getting warm. There was a long, long way to go. Stearns County was sort of like a church-state—"a lot more church than state," some said—where even the hardest of facts, the most damning of evidence might fail to break the iron vise of Faith.

9

The red International Harvester tractor was gone, but two equally distinctive vehicles graced the curb in front of the Goose Step Inn: Roy Riley's black van and Melvin Loftis' green GMC pickup. The singer's presence was signaled much more colorfully by his rhythmic, panting yowl, which, backed by throbbing guitars and a pounding drum, drifted out into Main Street.

Emil opened the door, stepped into the flashing lights, colored grime, and echoing din of the Goose Step. Melvin and the Long Prairie Boys were rehearsing a few new numbers on the tiny stage, Melvin sucking on the mike in his patented manner, jerking his guitar, a gaggle of afternooners looking on from barstools.

"Hey, Emil!" Melvin hollered when he caught sight of the old sheriff coming in.

The Boys did half a bar, realized Melvin had stopped caterwauling, and let the music die. Waves of electrified sound ebbed slowly, bounding and resounding from plank floor to tiled ceiling, paneled wall to paneled wall, shivering the bottles of booze lining the mirror behind the bar.

Loftis hopped down from the stage, flipped back layers of styled hair, and came across the dance floor to shake Emil's hand. If this morning's conversation in Corky's office had bothered him, he'd certainly managed to shrug it off easily enough.

"Take five, you guys," Melvin yelled to The Long Prairie Boys. "Sheriff, what're you drinking? It's on me."

The bar was big, made of dark, varnished wood. It ran

along one entire wall of the Goose Step, which was more the size of a small dance hall than a tavern. The walls were lined with high-backed booths, also of varnished wood. At the bar were a farmer and his wife, both of them sipping fifty-cent glasses of Hamm's beer, a truck driver, and three young women who seemed to belong to the boys in the band. Roy Riley lifted a can of Budweiser and winked at Emil, and a sales representative of Reuben's Beverages, who wore a company coverall and a softball cap, waved and said "Hi." He and Axel Vogel were eating cheese-burgers.

Standing behind the bar was a very pretty young girl who kept her eyes on Loftis, watching him as he moved. She had longish red hair, not frizzy Irish-orange but rich, sleek, and dark. She wore a green sweater that, as Sarah Whippletree would have said, "showed off her figure." When Emil slid up on to a bar stool, he could also see that she was wearing a little white apron and a pair of jeans that hugged two of the most provocative buttocks Whippletree had ever seen.

"Sheriff, this's Tulip Mosey," Melvin said.

Whippletree nodded. Tulip smiled.

She shouldn't have. Tulip had the body of a starlet, the face of the girl next door, but a set of teeth that would have kept an orthodontist in clover for a long, long time. Her eyes were dull-green and dreamy.

Whippletree made his estimate. Tulip was not the girl next door, but rather the girl down the street, halfway down the block, who skirts the edges of serious mischief in childhood, and lifts her skirts pretty soon thereafter. By the age of fifteen, she can glance into a car—any car, even a sportscar—and calculate at least half a dozen comforta-ble positions, some of which require her feet on the dash-board, the better for leverage and thrust.

"Nice to meet you, Miss Mosey," Emil said.

"It's Ms. What'll you have, Sheriff?"

"Whatever you want, Emil," Loftis declared expansively.

"How about a brandy?"

"C'mon, Sheriff. Have a whiskey, at least. It's almost Christmas time. Put a little heat in the blood."

"No thanks, just a brandy."

Tulip poured it and set it before him. "You want to question me now?" she asked. "I'm all ready."

"She's all ready," Melvin corroborated.

Emil took a swallow of brandy. It was cold. Should have ordered a toddy, but that might have been too complicated for the Goose Step.

"I was Trixie Miggs' best friend," Tulip said.

Whippletree took another sip of the brandy and looked around. "We can't talk here. How about we go over to one of those booths?"

Tulip brightened. Emil had never seen anybody so eager to be interrogated. Taking off the apron, she handed it to Loftis. "You take the bar for a little, okay, hon?" and, rear end twitching, led Emil to a booth in the far corner.

"We gonna be here a long time, Emil?" Axel Vogel asked. "Maybe I ought to radio back to the office?"

"Bring the car over here." Emil told him. "Eugenio Spritzer might want to move his Lincoln."

"Oh, is he over there seeing Father Creedmore again?" sniffed Tulip disgustedly, sliding into the booth.

Emil sat down across from her, sipped brandy, put down the glass. "You know Eugenio Spritzer? Wouldn't guess him to be your type. Does he come in here?"

"Come in *here?* He wouldn't come in here!"

"But you know him?"

"He's always in town. Sometimes he goes around passing out leaflets with pictures of dead babies on them. Most of the time, though, he sits over there in the rectory and looks out the window."

"What does he look at?"

"Anybody who comes in here. Mostly us girls."

"Well," Emil said, "let me ask you a couple of questions about the deaths of Mrs. Miggs and her boy."

"Poor Trixie." Tulip's eyes teared. She dried them with a little white paper napkin from the plastic dispenser there in the booth.

"As you probably know, your boyfriend's—"

"Fiancé," she corrected.

"—your fiancé's truck was seen around Mrs. Miggs' place, and he told the sheriff this morning that he was with you on the night of the murders."

Tulip nodded vigorously. "That's right. He was with me all night. It's all right, though, because we're gonna get married. Pretty soon. But he was with me, that's God's honest truth."

Emil believed her. "I don't want to stir up trouble between a couple of lovebirds, but I've heard that Melvin was seeing Trixie too."

"Oh, I know all about that. But it wasn't serious."

"Could you tell me the names of some of her other gentlemen?"

"Except for Melvin, they weren't gentlemen. No way. Let's see," Tulip unlimbered her fingers for counting, "there was that guy who drives the bread truck, Bawlie Wepner. And sometimes Flinch himself would come in here, talk to Trixie, and they would leave together, you know what I mean? Alf Toenjes, who plays bass guitar for Melvin, the one over there drinking tequila, he took Trixie out. And," Tulip lowered her voice, "that *Trib* reporter took her out too."

Riley? thought Emil, making a difficult but successful effort not to look in the reporter's direction. He remembered the picture of Trixie in the Indian costume, and the men behind her in the picture.

"Trixie ever go out with Sheriff Withers?" Emil asked.

Tulip gave a delicate little snort and smiled contemptuously. She had the right set of teeth for that kind of smile. "I think he was dying to ask her out. He had a habit, lately, of hanging around here and waiting till she came in so he could watch her dance. But he's one of those guys who can't get up the nerve to make a move."

"How do you know?"

"Women can tell."

"I see. Well, in your personal estimation, would any of the men you mentioned have reason to murder Trixie? And if so, would they be capable of doing it?"

Tulip's answer was immediate. "Flinch, yes," she said. "Bawlie Wepner, maybe. When he gets drunk he's not even a human being anymore. But he's sweet when he's sober. Alf the guitarist, never. He's gay, and I don't know anything about the reporter except that he uses words I don't understand."

"Like what?"

"I don't know. I forget. Like I say, I can't understand them, so why listen?"

"All right, now just a few more questions."

Axel Vogel came lumbering back inside. "Got a message for you Emil, soon as you're through there."

"Sure thing. Now, Ms. Mosey, I want you to keep in strictest confidence what I'm about to ask."

She leaned forward conspiratorially. "I'm real good at secrets, Sheriff."

"Was there any bad feeling between Trixie and Father Creedmore?"

Tulip sat back quickly. "Was there?" she asked. "*Was* there? It's all over town. But you don't think that *Father—?*"

"Shhhhh." He raised his hand. "What's all over town?"

"It was last Saturday," she whispered. "Trixie was over at the church standing in line to go to confession, on account of wanting to take Holy Communion at midnight Mass, you know? She had just come back from The Cities—"

"Why had she gone down there?"

"I don't know. Christmas shopping maybe. She didn't tell me. But, anyway, she was standing in line and then her turn came and she went into the confessional. All of a sudden, Father started yelling and shouting, bawling her out, you know? And then Trixie comes flying out of the confessional, really upset. Father Creedmore sticks his head out and yells at her, 'Come back here!' She stops and looks at him. 'You haven't gotten absolution yet,' he tells her. 'I don't want it from you,' she shouts at him, and runs out of the church. 'You'll never get it from anybody,' he yells after her. I mean, really. It was the talk of the town."

"Is Father Creedmore in the habit of doing that kind of thing? Yelling at people in the confessional?"

"Oh, yes. He yelled at me once, years ago." She giggled.

"What about, if it's not an intrusion?"

"I was pretty young. I did some things with a boy." She giggled again. "It was nothing important, but it seemed that way at the time. Father yelled and yelled. I thought I'd die, having to come out of the confessional with all those people looking at me."

"Well, Ms. Mosey. I'll report back to Sheriff Withers that you have an alibi for Melvin. Thanks for your time.

Emil felt very grateful to Tulip. And he already had a pretty strong suspicion about Trixie's unabsolved sin.

He weaned Axel Vogel from a pitcher of beer, took a rain check on Melvin Loftis' offer of a free concert, and left the Goose Step Inn.

"Oh, yeah," Axel remembered, "I got a message for you. Your wife's been calling Corky's office."

Emil felt a flutter of alarm in the fine hairs at the back of his neck. "Why?"

"Well, from what I understand, she's been getting these

phone calls, there at your house. You know, somebody calls and then hangs up?"

Dammit! Whippletree thought. Was it Spritzer? Or "Aynimous," the letter writer? Or somebody else?

Emil and the deputy were just about to get into the patrol car when Roy Riley walked out of the Goose Step and stood on the street looking at them. Whippletree saw a wrestler in the man's cannonball build, a city-slicker coolness in the combined amusement and intelligence on Riley's hard, keen face. But his smile gave him an entirely different look.

"Where are you going now?" Riley asked.

"How'd you know I was here in Silverton?"

"I guessed."

Emil didn't believe him.

"I wanted to ask Father Creedmore some questions," Riley was saying, "but he won't see me. He saw you though. What'd he say?"

"Not much."

"Is Father Creedmore a suspect in the murders?"

"I haven't the slightest idea."

"The priest's LeBaron was at the Miggs house almost at the very time the murders were committed and he's *not* a suspect? Isn't that unusual? Do you know anything about Father Peter Creedmore?"

"He's a Stearns County boy. Folks used to live and farm around St. Stephen. Went to Pater Noster Abbey, got ordained, and that's about it."

"Emil," said Riley, stepping close and speaking softly so that Axel Vogel couldn't hear, "do you want to take a look at Creedmore's bio sheet? I found it in the *Trib* files. Just between the two of us," he added.

"Doesn't pay not to look at free information," Emil said. "Is it important?"

"You'll have to tell me. You're the one who's lived here all your life."

"Well, bring it over to the house, or give me a call. But not till tomorrow. I got to go out shopping for a Christmas tree soon as I get back to town."

"Thanks, Emil," Riley said.

"What'd he want?" wondered Axel Vogel, driving back toward St. Cloud.

"He thinks you're the murderer, Axel. It'll be in the paper tomorrow morning."

Axel thought that over from a lot of angles. "Hell, it couldn't of been me," he assured Emil. "I spent that whole night humping the daylights out of Tulip Mosey."

Emil started in amazement and Axel roared. "Trying to pull my leg there, wasn't you, Emil? Just getting you back, is all. God, but I'd like to spend a month in Tulip's flower patch."

"She's already got a gardener."

"Yeah. Loftis. Shee-it, I think he's queer as a three-dollar bill. He can't sing, neither. The last good music to come out of this county was Elwood and the Blue Men. Remember 'em? They all had their hair dyed blue? Old Elwood. If you woulda closed your eyes you woulda thought he was Hank Williams. Whatever happened to old Elwood, anyway?"

"I think he delivers and installs for Kane's Karpet Kingdom, out on West Division Street."

"Too bad," sighed Axel. "Too fucking bad. That Elwood sure could sing. I really thought he was gonna go places."

They arrived back in St. Cloud at a little after four. Axel took the old sheriff straight to his house. Sarah was aggravated, but in no distress.

"Emil, the phone kept ringing. I'd answer it and there'd be somebody on the other end, just listening. It happened four times, one after the other. I called Corky's office and then took the phone off the hook."

"Still off?"

Sarah nodded. Emil limped into the kitchen and put the

receiver back in its cradle. Immediately, the phone rang. He lifted the receiver to his ear, but said nothing. Whoever it was on the other end didn't say anything either.

"Hey, Eugenio," said Emil, "you're a little punk in more ways than one."

"Emil?"

"Corky?"

"Yeah, it's me, Emil. What's going on there?"

"Those phone calls Sarah's been getting. I had an idea who was doing it. Forget it, for now."

"How did things go with Father Creedmore?"

Emil pulled out his notepad and read Corky the priest's guarded statement.

"That's terrific," Corky said. "I knew all along he was innocent."

"I think just the opposite. I think he's our man and that he's already desperate. He's also being protected by a rather powerful person here in the county, but I won't name names. I asked Creedmore how he'd feel about taking a polygraph test."

"But, we already *have* the killer. Flinch Miggs is the killer. He's got himself a lawyer now—Tricky Ricky Stein from Apple Valley—and Miggs wants a lie detector test right away. Stein is advising against it, though, so I guess *he* knows who the killer is."

"Corky, you know polygraph tests aren't admissible in court. Neither are those new stress detectors that measure the strain in your voice. But both of them, especially the poly, can give a guy a general idea of where there's smoke."

"A priest doesn't lie," Corky declared.

"I'm glad you said that. It means you were the one who allowed everything to be moved around in the murder house."

"What?" cried Corky, shaken and dismayed.

"That's exactly what Creedmore told me. He said you approved moving the bodies."

"There must be some mistake. You must have misunderstood Father."

"Nope."

"God, I—it's *not* true. But I don't know what . . . this, after everything else, and KSTP too."

KSTP was a Minneapolis TV station. "What about it?" Emil asked.

"Potoff and Fruth, those Bureau of Criminal Apprehension guys? They must have blabbed to the media. A camera team from KSTP is coming up here tomorrow to do a story on the murders. They want to talk to me."

"You think you'll fall on your face, don't you?"

"I didn't say *that*," said Corky.

"Look, Sheriff, go take a gander in the mirror. You'll do fine on TV. You'll do all right in this murder case too, *if* you check out every angle. If Creedmore's not guilty, nobody'll be more relieved than me. But serious evidence points to him, and you've got to follow it up."

Corky was quiet again. "Emil?" he asked after a moment, in a thin voice. "Emil, you know that, ah, undergarment? That was missing in the picture of Trixie's room? I was the one who moved it."

"Oh, Jesus Christ, Corky."

"I just put it in the laundry bag hanging behind the bedroom door. Really, I swear I did."

"Why the hell would you do that?"

"It didn't look nice lying there. It made her seem like a bad woman. So I put it in the bag. I'm telling the truth. I mean, I didn't take it home with me or anything."

"You had a case for Trixie Miggs, didn't you?"

"Yes," Corky admitted dolefully.

"Okay. If the subject of those panties comes up, you'll have to take the heat."

"All right, Emil. You sure I'll do fine on KSTP?"

"What was that about panties?" asked Sarah, after Emil had hung up.

"Hot stuff," he told her. "Can't talk about it."

"Hmmmmmmm. Are you ready to go get the Christmas tree now?"

"Here's my car key. Would you start the car and warm it up? Please? I have two quick calls to make."

Sarah went outside to start the car. She didn't drive, but he'd taught her how to get the engine running. He looked up a number in the book, and dialed. Elvira Heiderscheidt answered. "Emil," she cried, when he identified himself, "it's been a long time. I read about you in the paper. My, those awful murders."

"How's Mott?"

"Not too well, Emil. Not too well. It won't be long now, I'm afraid. He drifts in and out, but I think he'd like to see you one more time."

"I'll be out, Elvira. Promise. I understand Father Creedmore gave Mott last rites the other night?"

"Yes. It was so thoughtful of Father. Funniest thing. I didn't call him. He just came to the house at about three-thirty in the morning. He'd 'had a feeling,' he said. How about that?"

"How about that? Tell Mott I'll try and get out there."

Next, Emil called Doc Divot, the coroner. "Doc, on this Miggs thing," he said, "what're you keeping off the record?"

Percival Divot protested and sputtered.

"This isn't another Father Ripulski case, is it?" demanded Emil, referring to the time Otto Ronsky shot Father in the head for messing with Ronsky's wife. Divot had judged that one a "heart attack."

"Nothing like that," the doc cried, offended.

"Or another Leffuk deal?" Polly Leffuk had gone and gotten herself knocked up by the son of a prominent family. Said son was not so eager to continue the relationship, so Polly swallowed rat poison. Suicides gave the county a bad name. Divot wrote "gastrointestinal trauma" on the death certificate.

"Well, nothing along those lines, not exactly, Emil."

"Come clean. I know your ways, and you know mine. Body hasn't even been buried yet. If I wanted to make a big fuss, I could. But I don't. That's why I'm calling you."

"All right, Emil. There didn't seem any reason to include it in the autopsy report, what with the terrible thing that had happened, but Mrs. Miggs had undergone a D and C a short time before her death. Dilatation and Curettage."

"Tell me in plain language."

"Well, Trixie had been pregnant and she'd had an abortion, maybe last week. She must have been about two months gone."

I was right about that confession, Emil thought.

So, Emil calculated, Trixie had been pregnant when she danced her dance in the Indian costume, Thanksgiving night at the Goose Step Inn.

With Corky Withers and Bawlie Wepner staring at her, mesmerized by her, hooked and stricken and gone. Mel Loftis, sucking the mike, looking too. Flinch Miggs out somewhere, fighting or shooting or wandering around Stearns County.

Who was the proud papa?

Who was the killer?

How much is absolution worth?

10

Sarah had chosen a lush, long-needled Norwegian Pine. "It'll smell wonderful in the house," she'd said. Emil came downstairs for breakfast, and the sweet, sharp fragrance of the undecorated tree filled the house with perfume, took him back, way back. He was in his father's house sixty-odd years ago, enchanted by the wonder of strange candles on a magic day. Sentimental old bastard, he chastised himself, and limped to the breakfast table.

Sarah poured him Sanka and spooned honeyed oatmeal into a bowl. "How much did you drink yesterday?" she asked.

"Not much. Some brandy."

"Look at the way you're walking," she worried. "Cold and alcohol are the worst things for that knee. Doc said."

"I'll take it easy today."

"We have so much to do. Oh, well, it always gets done, doesn't it?"

Emil ate his breakfast and waited for the crisp smack of the *Trib* on the door. He heard a knock instead.

Sarah answered, and there was Roy Riley. He came in and handed Emil the paper. "Big front page story on the murders," he said.

Emil took the paper, unfolded it, scanned the headlines. A girl named Muffy Huff had been named Miss Ice Fishing Queen at a banquet in the Holiday Inn. Some trucker from North Dakota had wrapped his eighteen-wheeler around a roadside silo—the *Trib* was big on traffic coverage—and had, in the process, destroyed a Hannorhed Bank billboard. YOU'RE NEVER DEAD AT HANNORHED was draped, like a ragged ribbon, upon the overturned cab. Christmas tree sales were off three percent.

"I don't see any story on the Miggs case," Whippletree said, looking up at Riley.

"Oh, my mistake. Check page twenty-two."

Emil did. No byline. Not even a headline. Just a tiny paragraph, like the "fillers" containing random information that only an insomniac would ever get around to reading.

> Formal investigation of the two murders near Silverton was concluded today. "We have our man in custody," said County Sheriff Courtney P. Withers, Jr. Felix Miggs, estranged husband of one victim, father of the other, is awaiting arraignment on charges of first-degree murder. "It's all over. The people of Stearns County can rest easy," Sheriff Withers said, refusing further comment so as not to prejudice the case.

"Well, well," said Whippletree, dumbfounded, "you didn't write much of a story there."

"I didn't write it." Riley reached into his coat pocket and took out a thick sheaf of papers with triple-spaced typewritten text. "This is the story I wrote. It was sabotaged. My editor had instructions from somebody. He wouldn't print a word."

Emil scanned the article quickly. Worded fairly, even cautiously, it seemed to Emil an accurate depiction of the Miggs case so far.

"Doesn't seem too wild a story to me." Emil shrugged.

"We have a phrase in Chicago: 'The fix is in.' I think the fix is in."

"What the hell," said Emil. "So they're going to dump the whole thing on Flinch Miggs because he has a shotgun and no alibi."

The phone rang and Sarah answered.

"Who *are* you?" she demanded, after a moment, with a trace of fear in her voice. Holding the receiver away from her ear, she looked at Emil and Riley. "Whoever it was said, 'Tell your husband that'll teach him who not to' "— she hesitated, blushed—" '*you-know-what* with . . .' "

"Man or woman?"

"Man."

"It's that goddamn Eugenio Spritzer," Emil said. "I'm sure of it. You may be right, Riley. The fix is in, and Spritzer's gloating. But there's no way to prove he's the one who made this call, or that he made those weirdo calls yesterday."

"If he calls again, you could trace it," Riley offered. "It can be done."

"Ah, the hell with it. Well, Riley, what are you gonna do?"

"I don't know. I've been taken off the crime beat."

"Any reason given?"

"None. My assignment for today is to interview the forthcoming president of the Rosary Society, who lives at this address."

"How about a nice hot cup of coffee?" Sarah offered. She set the cup and coffee pot, cream, and sugar on the table and excused herself to dress. "I don't want to be interviewed in a housecoat," she said.

Emil waited until his wife was upstairs, then he asked, "How was your date with Trixie Miggs?"

Riley, a little surprised, reached for his cigarettes. Marlboros. He lit one. "Not bad," he said.

"Thought you smoked Salems?"

"I smoke all kinds."

Emil could understand that. Sometimes he chewed Red

Man, sometimes Copenhagen, now and then Svobriskie. "So? About Trixie?"

"I went out with Mrs. Miggs a couple of times," Riley admitted.

"What happened?"

"We fucked. We didn't show any affection, we didn't entertain each other, we didn't even get carried away by passion. We just fucked."

"How come only a couple of times?"

"She started hanging around with Bawlie, and then that singer, Loftis."

"Gave you the cold shoulder?"

"She gave me cold everything."

"Woman like that, though, she *could* get under a man's skin?"

Riley exhaled cigarette smoke and checked the staircase to make sure Sarah wasn't on her way down. "Sheriff, you have no idea. She could pump a man dry in ten minutes and leave him lying in the ditch at the side of the road."

Hardly the type of woman to make a big thing out of going to confession, Emil reasoned. Unless Trixie had done something so serious that it appalled even her. And Emil knew that she had. The worst thing a Stearns County Catholic girl *could* do. That was the substance of her Christmas confession to Father Peter Creedmore.

So that was why he *killed* her? Some insane brand of right-to-life revenge?

"Oh, by the way," said Riley, "here's that bio data on Creedmore I said I'd bring over." He handed Emil a sheet of photocopied material.

Sarah came downstairs, all dressed up, wearing high heels, looking nervous. She and Riley went out into the living room. Emil studied the cryptic record of Father Creedmore's life.

CREEDMORE, PETER JOHN THOMAS

Pastor, St. Hrothgar's church, Silverton, MN., 1978–present

D.o.b. April 1, 1935

Education: Holy Mother of Mercy School, St. Stephen, 1941–46;

  Pater Noster Abbey School, 1946–49;

  Pater Noster Abbey Preparatory School, 1949–1953;

  Pater Noster Abbey College and Divinity School, 1953–1961.

Ordained to the priesthood: June 1, 1961.

Assignments: Assistant Pastor, St. Cloud Cathedral Parish, 1961–68.

St. Concepta's Mental Health Institute, Big Falls, 1968–70. Chaplain.

Catholic University, Washington, D.C. Instructor in Sacred Theology, 1970–75.

Assistant Pastor, St. Cloud Cathedral Parish, 1975–78.

In the living room, Whippletree heard Roy Riley asking Sarah all about her life and interests. She had warmed up to the interview and was talking easily now. Riley was doubtless using his smile. Emil listened, pleased. Now and then Sarah mentioned his name, saying things like "those years we had it tough, farming, just married, and Emil putting his brother, Hugh, through school" and "now that was the year Emil first ran for sheriff . . ."

He looked again at the data sheet on Father Creedmore, trying to get a mental fix on the guy. Farm boy, one of thousands in Stearns County. But some yearning flicker of intelligence or desire had set little Peter apart. At eleven years of age, he had left the farm for good, called by God. Pater Noster took boys when they were very young, to make priests of them behind stone walls and Prairie-Gothic battlements. Childhood, adolescence, and young manhood expended apart from the world, in piety

and rigor, self-denial and renunciation, flagellation, abne-
gation and . . . hope.

A couple of things on Creedmore's résumé puzzled
Emil. Back there in 1961, the guy comes out of seminary
and gets assigned assistant pastor at the big church, the
Cathedral. A lot of the young guys got assigned there. It
was a large parish and needed a lot of priests to hear
confessions, say masses, listen to people's problems. Then
he goes to the mental home as chaplain, on to be a professor at Catholic U.—no Stearns County Syndrome in Peter
Creedmore—and after all that experience he comes back
to the Cathedral as an assistant pastor again.

Why would he want to do that?

More accurately, who would make him do it?

There was only one answer: Wilhelm Theobald Bundeswehr, bishop of Stearns County. Those priests didn't even
go from one town to another without his blessing, let
alone all the way to Washington, D.C.

Sarah and Roy Riley came back into the kitchen, Riley
closing the cardboard cover on his notepad and putting it
into his pocket.

"You have an accomplished wife here, Emil," he said.

"I've known that for a hell of a long time."

"Watch your language," said Sarah, beaming.

Riley helped himself to a second cup of coffee. Emil told
him what he'd like to know about Father Creedmore.

"Easy," said the reporter. "May I use your phone?"

He dialed. "Operator, would you please give me the
number of St. Concepta's Mental Health Institute in Big
Falls. . . .

"Good morning. This is Mr. Roy Riley, of the St. Cloud
Morning Tribune. May I speak to the superintendent
please? I'm thinking of doing a story and—thank you, yes,
I'll hold."

He winked at Emil. "Well, I'm always thinking of doing
one story or another."

"Hello? Sister Assumption? Good morning. Roy Riley,

of the *Trib*. Down here in St. Cloud. I'm considering a story, something on the order of 'Chaplains of St. Concepta.' They do hard work and—yes, yes, I agree. So, if you'd be so kind, would you help out by giving me the names of chaplains you've had there for, oh, say the past twenty years?" Riley made a circle with thumb and forefinger.

"Yes, sister, I have a pencil," said Riley, who did not.

He listened for a time. "Thank you, Sister. Thank you so much. I'll be in contact with these individuals. Oh, wait, let's see, isn't Father Peter Creedmore missing from the list you gave me?"

He listened some more, slightly tense at the phone now.

"Oh, I see. My mistake. Of course, I understand. I couldn't agree with you more."

After several more thank yous, Riley hung up.

"What did she say?" Emil asked. "About Creedmore?"

The reporter gave him a straight look. "She said they never release information on patients."

Emil looked at the data sheet again. "After his two years in St. Concepta's, Father Creedmore lived for five years in Washington, D.C."

Riley sat down at the table, and pursued Emil's train of thought. "And I bet he wasn't spending much time teaching Sacred Theology at Catholic U., either. I ought to have been bright enough to catch that before. The guy's got no publications, no specialized degrees. And he comes back here to Stearns County, takes up the routine of a parish priest."

"I wonder where in D.C. he received treatment?" Emil mused. "Well, doesn't much matter. Creedmore's whole life is suspect now."

Sarah, who had listened in puzzlement while Riley wiled his way with Sister Assumption, showed faint alarm. "What is all this about poor Father Creedmore? He was in a mental institution?"

"I think he killed Mrs. Miggs and her son."

"Emil—no! Why?"

"It has to do with confession, abortion, maybe just the way she affected him. I don't know yet."

"Abortion!" gasped Sarah.

"Hate to say it, but it looks that way. I just wonder where in Minneapolis she had it done."

"Poor girl," observed Riley. "Doubt she'd go to a private physician. A clinic is more likely."

"Willow Creek," exclaimed Sarah.

"Sure," Riley agreed. "It's a possibility. That's the planned parenthood center in Bloomington, not far from the stadium. Some Right-to-Lifer fire-bombed the place once."

Emil made the call this time. Special Deputy Emil Whippletree investigating a murder in which Father Peter Creedmore might have been involved.

The name Creedmore made quite an impact at the Willow Creek Center. Officials there would be cooperative. Character witnesses, in a manner of speaking. But they wouldn't do it over the phone. Emil made an appointment for eleven and said good-bye.

He checked the kitchen clock. Almost eight-thirty.

"I can make it easy," he said. "And probably be back before three this afternoon."

"Mind if I come along?" Riley asked. "I'll drive."

"You're on," said Emil.

11

Before heading down to Bloomington, Emil asked Roy Riley to stop at the jail. "I want to see what's going on," he said.

Alyce was at her desk in the outer office. Corky's office door was closed, as was the door to the cellblock. Flinch and the other guests were quiet, but from Corky's office came frequent bursts of passionate conviction.

"Who's he talking to?" Emil asked.

"Nobody. He's in there alone, rehearsing what he'll say when KSTP-TV shows up."

"What's he going to say?"

"I don't know. He went through about eight or nine little speeches. He's back on the first one now."

"Any late stuff on the Miggs case?"

Alyce checked a pile of papers on her desk. "We got a confirmation from Mr. Potoff of the BCA. All fingerprints in the house have been accounted for, except that set of prints on the guns found in the Miggs' closet. Where you headed?"

Emil was going to tell her Minneapolis, but held back. "Here and there," he said.

"But I saw you get out of Roy Riley's van?"

"So? I was just trying out his waterbed."

"Oh, Emil, g'wan. There isn't no waterbed in there."

"And Riley told me he's going to ask you out on a date."

Alyce's mouth flew open. "He's going to—he can't do that! Why, I'm married!"

"Doesn't matter to him. He's from Chicago. He told me it's more fun when it's illicit."

"Well, you tell him—" sputtered Alyce, incensed.

"Okay, but I got to run now. See you later."

"Anything happening in there?" asked Riley, as he pulled away from the curb.

"Corky's talking to himself and Alyce said she wants a date with you."

"Dangerous. Last woman I dated got her head blown off."

They drove southward out of St. Cloud and swung onto I-94 near St. Augusta. Home of the "Gussies," who were forever locked in deadly horsehide rivalry with the Luxemburg "Lux." Old men could tell you what had happened in the bottom of the third inning in a game played thirty years ago.

The big engine in Riley's van had them flying along, past Clearwater and Monticello. Skies were dull gray, and occasional flurries of snowflakes lanced into the windshield like white angry gnats. Stripped trees were black and stark against fields of old snow, and the lakes along the roadside were pale and lustreless.

"Storm by nightfall," Emil observed, studying the sky. "Predicted her yesterday."

"How can you tell?"

"Change in the air. I can smell it. Sky comes down real low."

"Well, if it comes early and traps us at roadside, don't worry." Riley patted the dashboard. "This baby will take care of us. Heat, food, whatever. If we're snowbound, we could easily last a week, or until the plows get through."

Emil examined the dashboard, with its flashing array of panels and switches and dials.

"How'd you get interested in this kind of thing?"

"Down in Chicago. I was interested in science. Won a national science fair award for transistors. Now I'm using silicon chips."

"What can you do with them?" Emil asked.

"Well, if I wanted to, I could—" Riley paused. "Emil,

remember the Pueblo? That communications ship captured by the North Koreans? It was anchored off the Korean coast, picking up information from their airwave and electronic transmissions."

"Sure do."

"*If* I wanted to I could, say, park my van outside a—just for example, a rectory—turn on a piece of equipment and, by picking up dialing signals, determine the exact phone numbers dialed from the rectory phone."

"I see," said Emil. "This rectory could be anywhere, couldn't it? Maybe right across the street from a roadhouse? And a number of calls could have been made from that rectory to . . ." He gave his home number.

"Could happen. Speaking hypothetically, of course."

"Son of a bitch," Emil said. "I *knew* it.

"I wonder who got Trixie Miggs pregnant?" he asked, after a minute.

"It wasn't me! They cut down the pleasure, but I use them. You can catch herpes from a homegrown cornfed girl as easily as from a South Side hooker."

They drove on in silence for a mile or two, the wind howling outside the van.

"Maybe it was Creedmore," Riley suggested abruptly.

"But Trixie and *Father Creedmore?*" The possibility had not occurred to Whippletree at all. What if . . . what *if* Trixie had conceived and aborted the priest's child? And what if she'd threatened to tell about it? In that case, wouldn't somebody want to shut her mouth? And if that somebody happened to be Peter Creedmore, wouldn't Bishop Bundeswehr be inclined to keep the lid on?

Bundeswehr had not hesitated to do exactly that when Otto Ronsky killed Father Ripulski in a cornfield. Bundeswehr had even tried to excommunicate a farmer once. He was capable of plenty.

"You'd be surprised at how many women fantasize about making it with men of God," Riley was saying. "Psychologically, it's the supreme proof of their womanhood. To be more compelling than God. Why do you think *The Thorn Birds* was so popular?"

"But Father Creedmore and *Trixie?*" Emil said doubtfully. "We're not talking Richard Chamberlain here."

"Creedmore was seen there at the time of the murders. His behavior in the house was strange, messing with the evidence and all that. And, clearly, he's not only being protected by the Chancery, he's got a weird friend who's harassing you and your wife."

"Yeah, Spritzer."

Josh Miggs had said that the man in the doorway with the shotgun was big. Spritzer was not. But, to a kid lying on a mattress on the floor, wouldn't almost any upright figure look pretty tall? Especially in the darkness by a flash of blue light?

"Son of a bitch," he said again.

Suddenly, Emil was pushed back into his cushioned bucket seat. Riley stamped down on the accelerator and the van shot forward. The legal fifty-five miles per hour was left far behind. Ninety miles an hour, then ninety-five.

Just as abruptly as he had accelerated, Riley now braked, skidded beneath an overpass, reversed and backed furiously, tires scattering gravel, pebbles, snow, and ice. The van came to a jolting stop behind a huge concrete abutment supporting the overpass, where the Highway Patrol liked to wait for speeders.

"What in hell . . . ?" Emil was glad he had a seatbelt on. Riley didn't say a word.

Ten seconds later, maybe fifteen, a big blue Lincoln flashed by, and Whippletree glimpsed, momentarily, the slight figure crouched behind the wheel. "By God, it's Eugenio Spritzer," he said, amazed.

"I recognized the car from the rectory yesterday. I think he picked us up in St. Cloud, when we made the turn at the Dippi-Freez. Followed us all the way. What does Spritzer do? When he's not hanging around the rectory in Silverton?"

"He's lay director of the Life Saviors."

"I know that. But what does he *do*? He's got that expensive car and he's obviously got a lot of time on his hands. He used to be an orderly at St. Concepta's Home. Spritzer's people have money?" Riley asked.

"Unlikely. If they do, it's invested in tractors, combines, and irrigation equipment. Not Lincolns."

"Spritzer's got a Lincoln," Riley said.

12

Willow Creek Planned Parenthood Clinic was a one-story beige-brick affair, larger than Whippletree had imagined. It was set back from the street, and a new chain-link fence separated clinic property from the sidewalk running around it. A muscular young man stood guard at a gate in the fence, looking casually bored as a half-dozen women in parkas and boots tromped up and down in the snow, carrying hand-lettered placards that read MURDER FACTORY and A NEW EINSTEIN MAY DIE HERE TODAY and STOP THE DEATH MERCHANTS.

Whippletree gave his name to the guard. He and Riley went through the gate, up the walk, and into the clinic. The waiting room was occupied by at least fifty people, most of them women, maybe a half-dozen men, and two teenage boys who looked as anxious as the young women with them. The atmosphere was quiet, with a sharp touch of tension. The receptionist behind a plastic window told Whippletree that Dr. Bradley was expecting him, and led him down a long, many-doored corridor. Riley followed. They were shown to an austere office with a gunmetal gray desk, a rank of metal files along one wall, and a cluster of folding chairs set up near a small movie projector. A lovely but tired-looking young woman was riffling through a drawerful of files. The receptionist retreated. Emil wondered where the doctor was. The young woman told him.

"I'm Sharon Bradley," she said. "Which one of you is Mr. Whippletree?"

"I am," said Emil. "Special duty from Stearns County."

Dr. Bradley glanced inquiringly at Roy Riley.

"I'm a reporter with the St. Cloud *Morning Tribune*. Just came along for the ride. Guess you want me to leave, huh?"

She smiled, and the fatigue left her face momentarily. Whippletree was a little startled, not because such a young woman was a doctor, but that a doctor could be so pretty.

"It's perfectly all right, Mr. Riley," she said. "I believe this meeting is to be about Peter Creedmore. I want as many people as possible to see what Peter Creedmore is like. Mr. Whippletree, you mentioned in your phone call that you are investigating a case of some kind in which Creedmore is involved?"

"It's a murder case." Whippletree watched her face closely as he spoke. "A woman named Trixie Miggs was killed near St. Cloud the other morning, and we have reason to believe Father Creedmore might have been involved. Was Mrs. Miggs a patient at this clinic?" he asked.

Dr. Bradley had obviously made up her mind about him. "Mrs. Miggs was a patient."

"For consultation or for . . . other?"

"Not just for consultation. Do you think Father Creedmore killed her?"

"Don't know. I started to figure there was some connection between Trixie Miggs and your clinic, and then I learned that the Stearns County Life Saviors had done some picketing here."

"*Some* picketing? They're *always* here. I think they're the group that firebombed us just last month, although I can't prove anything. But I want you to watch this."

Dr. Bradley stepped to the projector. "Would one of you turn out the lights please?"

Riley did so, and the doctor switched on the machine.

A square of white light appeared on the opposite wall.

"We'd been having trouble for so long that I decided enough was enough and ordered all demonstrations filmed."

A crowd of people, slightly out of focus, appeared on the wall. Dr. Bradley adjusted the machine. "This was filmed just before Thanksgiving by a member of my staff."

The staff member could have stood a couple of courses in cinematography, but the product was adequate to its purpose. The scene on camera showed the metal fence outside the clinic, and the young man standing guard at the gate. There was a major demonstration going on outside the fence, with fully a hundred people milling on the sidewalk and spilling into the street. A forest of red-lettered placards rose above the heads of the crowd, showing pictures of blood-dripping fetuses and the usual passionate slogans.

"Keep your eyes open," Dr. Bradley said.

The camera panned slowly along the fence, where Spritzer and Father Creedmore were standing. Spritzer stared at the camera, then grinned. The priest faced a crowd of demonstrators, his arms moving rhythmically, leading a chant. The mouths of the demonstrators opened and closed. Placards swayed from side to side. Spritzer said something to the guard at the gate, who turned quickly toward the little man. Spritzer said something else. The guard shrugged.

A woman left the clinic and approached the gate. Her back was visible to the camera. The guard saw her coming and swung the gate open. He looked tense. The demonstrators forgot about Creedmore's chant and began to shout at the woman. Creedmore and Eugenio looked at each other and edged toward the open gate. The woman walked through the gate. Demonstrators parted reluctantly, letting her pass. They kept on shouting at her, though, some of them leaning close and peering at her. Angry faces. The woman ran a gauntlet of rage.

"Just keep watching," Dr. Bradley said.

Now another woman, quite young, came through the crowd and approached the gate, which was still open. The demonstrators shrieked at her. Father Creedmore was at the gate now. She looked at the burly priest in fearful surprise, turned sideways and slipped past him. The guard lunged at Creedmore, who tried to grab the woman. Dr. Bradley stopped the film to show Father Creedmore's face, frozen in a rictus of fury. Then the film rolled again, showing the terrified woman running up the walk toward the clinic. The guard grabbed Creedmore's shoulder but Eugenio Spritzer pulled his arm away. Creedmore pursued the woman, a triumphant expression on his face as his fingers closed around the collar of her coat. Her mouth flew open and she screamed. The priest's thick arm went around her waist. Demonstrators shouted and waved their placards. Spritzer tried to hold on to the guard. He was shaken off and pushed into the fence. Creedmore had both arms around the woman now, trying to wrestle her to the ground. The guard ran forward and pulled the priest off her. Creedmore drew back his right arm, his hand in a fist. The guard struck him hard and clean on the left side of the jaw. He spun around and fell.

Three policemen, waving billy clubs, charged through the gate. The screen went white. The projector motor hummed in the little office. Roy Riley turned on the lights, and Dr. Bradley switched off the machine.

"Well," she asked, "how's that for evidence?"

"Doesn't show murder," said Emil.

"But an excellent character study," the reporter observed. "What happened afterward?"

"Well, our patient filed assault charges. But, to my regret, she never carried through."

"To your regret?"

"You saw the film. Creedmore is a sick man. He could be extremely dangerous. But our patient just didn't have the strength to bear the inevitable publicity a trial would have brought, so the charges were withdrawn."

"What about Father Creedmore?"

"He spent a night in Hennepin County Jail."

"And you were firebombed that night?" asked Emil.

"Yes," said Sharon Bradley. "Some damage. We had to close down three examining rooms for a month."

Creedmore couldn't have firebombed anything from a jail cell, figured Emil. But Spritzer might have.

13

"**W**ell, Emil," called Riley from the back of the van, "if Creedmore comes to trial for killing Trixie, you might get Dr. Bradley's film introduced as evidence."

"Hell, the way things are going, Creedmore will never come to trial at all. Bishop Bundeswehr is going to block any approach to Creedmore, and Corky will keep trying to hang the murders on Flinch Miggs."

Emil was driving the van to St. Cloud and Riley was at work in the back. The typewriter clattered, fell silent, and clattered again. He was writing the piece on Sarah.

No big snow yet, it was coming, but they'd get home all right. Emil was trying to think about the Miggs case as he drove, but something kept intruding, kept nudging his mind away from the murders. He didn't know what it was for a long time, as Roy Riley cursed and clacked and clattered at his typewriter. It was a feeling Emil had known a long, long time ago. So long ago, in fact, he doubted its resurgence. But he held with the impulses, did not turn them aside, and put them together piece by piece as he drove. The conclusion, when it came, was a knockout: he felt young again. What do you know, devil take it, he felt *young* again! Here he was, retired old codger, out on an adventure with a smart young guy who was teaching him things and who—Emil was pretty sure—didn't mind his company a bit, might even be finding it worthwhile. Emil's cane lay on the floor, there were liver spots on his gnarled hands, and beneath his waistband he could feel the itch of dry skin that plagued him in the winter. So what? he thought. I'm not through yet.

"I just came up with a notion," he called to Riley. "If we can't bell the cat, we've got to maneuver him into doing it himself."

"Creedmore?"

"Right. How would you feel if you'd killed somebody?"

Riley thought it over. "To be honest, if it was somebody I'd really hated, I don't know."

"What if you'd done it and you thought everybody knew? All your neighbors. All your friends. Everybody. What if you were going out of your mind with guilt on the one hand and the knowledge that *everybody knew* on the other?"

"I guess I wouldn't feel too good. What have you got in mind?"

"If the Church and the law won't do their jobs and bring Father Creedmore in," Emil said, "then the only way left open is to drive Creedmore to a confession."

"Okay, but how are you going to do it?"

"Step by step. But one way or another, I'm going to. That man, even if he isn't a killer, shouldn't have a position of authority. That's what I concluded after I talked to him at the rectory, but I held back, gave him the benefit of the doubt. After seeing Dr. Bradley's film, though, I've got a lot more doubt and a lot less benefit."

A dark mid-afternoon, a mean wind, and the ubiquitous Hannorhed bank billboard welcomed Emil and Riley back to Stearns County. Riley was behind the wheel again, his article completed.

"How long have you been married, Sheriff?" Riley asked.

"Forty-six years. Forty-seven, come June."

"Wow! That's incredible, these days. How did it happen?"

"I don't know. One day at a time, I guess."

"Ever have fights? Things like that?"

"No, but we had a big silence once. That is, Sarah had a big silence. About thirty years ago. She didn't talk to me for three days, I think it was."

"What was that all about?"

Emil realized that, while he remembered the episode, he couldn't recall what had caused it.

"You got me. I forgot."

"But you've been happy?"

Emil shrugged. "I think so. I never gave it much thought. The one sure way to be unhappy is to worry about whether you're happy or not."

Riley took the Clearwater exit off I–94 and cut west over an unpaved road toward Silverton and Mott Heiderscheidt's place. The mounting wind, which had kept the expressway free of snow so far, was having the opposite effect here. Sheets of snow shot over piled banks alongside the road, drifting heavily. The van hit a big drift. The engine labored and roared.

"Maybe we should have stayed on the main road," Emil said apologetically.

"No sweat. We can make it."

Riley pulled into the Heiderscheidt's farmyard and elected to wait in the van while Emil made his sick call. A dispirited old mutt crawled out from beneath the farmhouse porch and gave a couple of gratuitous barks, his tail going like mad. The dog tried to jump up at Emil, begging for affection, but age prevented it. "Yeah, pooch, I know how it is," murmured the old sheriff, scratching the dog's bowed head lovingly.

Elvira Heiderscheidt answered his knock. "Emil, I knew you'd come."

"Can't stay long. There's a blizzard coming. Mott's awake?"

The house was very cold. Elvira led him through the kitchen, with its sagging, ancient cupboards and yellowed range, down a cold, narrow wallpaper-peeling hallway and into the bedroom. What remained of the boy Emil had grown up with, and the man he had known all his life, lay flat on his back in bed, bundled and tucked.

Mott's arms were under the covers. Emil rested his hand lightly on his friend's shoulder.

Mott's eyes flickered open. "Emil," he gasped drily, in recognition.

Death was here, and Emil sensed it. But it was not the species of Death he had divined at the Miggs house. That had been vicious, demonic; this was merely inevitable.

"How you doing, Mott?"

"Not so good. But I've made up my mind to last till Christmas."

"I'm going to set up a little tree," Elvira said. She stood beside Emil, next to the bed.

"Wouldn't you be better off in the hospital?" Emil asked.

Mott gave a dry, croaking laugh. "Don't want to die there. I can still decide that much."

"Just wanted to stop in and say hello."

"Good-bye, you mean. But thanks, Emil."

The two old men looked at each other, one at the end of his days, the other getting close. Emil's throat felt hot and tight. He didn't know what to say. "Well, we had us some good times," he said.

"We did," Mott agreed. Then he said, with effort, "Remember, Emil? Remember I told you to stay in the damn boat?"

"You did. And you were right."

Mott was referring to the time he and Nubs and Emil had commandeered Nubs' father's rowboat and gone out voyaging on Tufo's lake. Emil could still recall the pleasure of freedom, the quiet of surrounding woods, and a sense of accomplishment, feelings that dissolved very quickly when he felt the water start curling up around his ankles. The rowboat, warping and drying all summer, was shipping water like there was no tomorrow. Emil and his buddies realized there would *not* be a tomorrow if they didn't get back to shore awful quick, and the rowing was not so easy with all that extra weight of lakewater to haul along. "If we get out, the boat'll be lighter," Emil had suggested, "and we can pull her in to shore." Mott and Nubs had counseled against such rashness, due to the murky, sucking lake-bottom. But Emil, bold captain, felt a need to act, since they were telling him how stupid he had been to get them into such a mess in the first place.

Pretending confidence, and hoping for the best, Emil jumped out of the wallowing rowboat. And up to his waist in the water and the clutching muck beneath the water. Tales of quicksand were the hard currency of childhood terror—the smallest mud-puddle might veil a sinister pit of the stuff—and Emil went into a panic. The mud drew him down until water lapped at his chin. Losing his head, he lost his balance too, and fell beneath the surface, choking, flailing. He would surely have gone straightaway to hell, too, because he couldn't remember one word of the Act of Contrition he had learned in catechism class. Then he felt an arm around his neck and his head was above the water again. Nubs had jumped in after him.

Not until years afterward did Emil realize fully that Nubs Tufo had saved his life that day, and had thrown his own safety into jeopardy in the bargain. Emil had acted, but foolishly. Nubs had waited until he saw that there was nothing left to do, and then had acted, ending a bad situation by jumping into it the only way he knew how. Mott had stayed in the boat.

"How is Nubs?" Mott faltered, lying on his deathbed.

"About the same," Emil answered. "Gettin' old like me."

"Tell him—tell him Merry Christmas."

"I will."

Elvira took Emil back through the kitchen to the door.

"Nubs was here last week," she said. "A lot of the old guard are coming around."

"That's good. When we're gone, a way of life'll go with us. There'll be nobody left to remember what this country was like when it was new."

Elvira's pose of good cheer failed her for a moment. "Emil, I'm so tired."

He took her hand and held it for a long time.

"It was nice of Father Creedmore to come the other night. And just when he's been over that very afternoon, too. I guess I'll be calling him when the final crisis hits Mott."

She hadn't heard that Creedmore was a murder suspect. Emil wouldn't tell her.

"Three-thirty in the morning! Can you believe it?"

"Yes, I can believe it."

He said good-bye, taking Elvira's wishes to Sarah with him, and went outside. Snow, real snow, had begun to fall now. It made a hissing sound in the branches of trees and rattled like sleet against the black metal of Riley's van.

"You were right, Emil," the reporter said, "you've got your storm."

Riley wheeled the van around the farmyard and out to the road. "No problem yet," he said, crashing through a two-foot-high drift. "We'll cut over to Silverton and go right on in to St. Cloud."

Past the murder house, Emil thought. In a minute, the bright yellow ranch appeared on their left.

Bawlie Wepner's house looked shut and dark, but his Dough-Rite bakery truck was parked out front. Emil was just wondering if Bawlie might have fathered Trixie Miggs' aborted child when Nubs Tufo's battered old pickup hurtled from a side road and directly into the path of the van. Riley braked hard, and Emil was thrown forward into the dashboard. On an icy road, there would have been a collision for certain, but drifting snow cut the van's momentum. At the last moment, Nubs saw them coming, and swerved. The two vehicles came to a halt within feet of each other.

"Jesus!" cried Riley. "Emil are you okay?"

"I think so." He pushed himself back up into the bucket seat—got to remember to wear the belt, most accidents happen closest to home—and looked out the window. Nubs Tufo was climbing out of his truck, peering at the van. In the pickup's shotgun seat lolled Bawlie Wepner.

"Looks like Bawlie's hurt," said Emil.

"What the hell do you think you're doing?" roared Nubs, as Riley got out of the van. "Oh, hi, Emil."

Emil pulled up his collar, drew down the earflaps on his hat, and climbed out too. Snowflakes dived in and scoured his face. The air was cold and dry.

"Bawlie all right?" he asked, walking over to the truck.

The window on the passenger side of the truck was gone, and the paint around its door was pocked and scarred. Nubs had replaced the glass temporarily with a sheet of heavy, translucent plastic. Behind the plastic, Emil could see Bawlie Wepner, whose big body seemed to have lost most of its muscle control.

"Open the door careful, there," said Nubs, "else he's liable to fall out."

"Were you in an accident?" Riley asked him.

"Might say that. I was haulin' firewood, two, three days ago, ran into a low-hanging tree branch up on that hill behind my cabin, knocked out the whole damn window."

Carefully, he opened the truck door. Bawlie, leaning in that general direction, began a slow, sliding tilt. Nubs braced an arm against the former baseball pitcher's shoulder.

"Unnhh," Bawlie said, blinking a little. He had lost more than muscle control. A dark, sodden patch soiled his Dough-Rite coveralls in the area of the groin.

"What's the matter with him?" asked Riley, who didn't know the Wepner saga too well.

"He's drunk as a skunk is what's wrong with him," Nubs said. "I went into St. Cloud today to pick up a tombstone"—Emil glanced in the pickup's cargo box and, sure enough, there was a small polished granite stone with a chiselled name: STORMY—"and when I got back to the cabin, there was Wepner, sitting in my easy chair and trying to finish off a second quart of brandy. I bought the stuff for Christmas Tom and Jerries, too."

"Emil," groaned Bawlie, recognizing him, "unnnhhh."

"Anyway," Nubs said, "I got him into my truck and I'm taking him to his place. I'd appreciate a hand."

Emil couldn't do much, what with his bad leg, but Riley volunteered. Nubs drove the truck to Bawlie's door, where he and the reporter half carried, half dragged Wepner into his house and laid him down on the couch. He stank of liquor and urine.

"I'll see if I can find a blanket," Riley said, looking around the house, going back toward the bedrooms.

Nubs and Emil stood over Bawlie. "Shame to leave him here," Emil said.

"Well, I don't want him over at my place. He'll be all right. It's warm. He'll sleep it off."

"Emuhl," Bawlie slobbered. "The murd I—I knowgh—"

"Hey, good, Bawlie," Nubs said. "How come he shows up at my place everytime he goes on a jag?"

"I—Emuhl—"

"What'd he say?" asked Emil sharply.

"He ain't said a thing I could make sense of since I found him at my place."

"No, he said something about knowing who the killer is." Emil lowered himself stiff-jointedly and knelt beside the couch. So did Nubs.

"He has been blubbering on," Nubs admitted. "I didn't pay no attention."

Bawlie's eyes were closed now. His breath gurgled liquidly in his throat.

"Hey! Wepner!" said Nubs, shaking the man. "Wepner, what was that you said?"

Bawlie coughed and began to snore.

"Come on, Wepner," said Nubs, shaking him some more.

"Oh, let him alone," Emil said. "I'll give him a call in the morning. He's no use to us now."

Emil and Nubs got to their feet. "Think he might actually know something?" Nubs mused.

"You got me. Everybody in the county is a detective these days. Knowing Bawlie, it's probably liquor talking."

Riley came back with a couple of army blankets and spread them over the pitiful, mewling drunk.

"What the hell," Nubs said.

They decided little else could be done so, leaving Bawlie safe in his house, the three men went outside. It was snowing heavily now. "You boys better get on the road," Nubs said. "You can make 'er back to town if you go now."

"Sorry your dog died, Nubs," said Emil.

Tufo didn't say anything for a moment. "Had him with me for fourteen years," he said, sadly. "He was a good dog." He paused, uncertain whether or not to reveal further pain, then decided to risk it because Emil was a friend. "Losing him like that was awful bad, and now I don't know if I should get me a new dog or not. Don't know how long I'll be around, and if I croak there's the poor mutt left alone."

"Hell, Nubs, you'll last another twenty years, at least."

Nubs Tufo gave Emil a straight look. "No, I won't. There's too much water over the dam, and it won't come back."

Riley had the van humming and Emil climbed in. "Don't forget to drop by for them Tom and Jerries," Nubs called. "I'll buy more brandy."

"No, I'll bring some," Emil promised.

Driving through Silverton, he and Riley noticed Mel Loftis' GMC pickup parked in front of the Goose Step Inn. Across the street, Eugenio Spritzer's big blue Lincoln hunched beneath a couple of inches of snow. There were lights in the rectory windows.

"Well, Spritzer got back before we did," Riley observed. "I'm sure he was following us. Wonder if he picked up our trail after we ditched him at that underpass?"

Emil didn't say anything. He was thinking. If the little Life Savior suspected that Emil had made a connection involving abortion, Trixie Miggs, and Father Creedmore, all he would have needed for proof was to see Riley's black van parked outside the Willow Creek Clinic. If he had, words being spoken behind the rectory walls right now might scorch some ears.

"You have a machine to pick up conversations inside people's houses?" he asked Riley, only half jokingly.

The reporter laughed. "No. What my moral code might permit, my income won't. Why?"

"It would make things a lot easier."

Emil still believed that Creedmore had killed Trixie Miggs, but now, as Riley drove, the old sheriff turned his attention to the personality and behavior of Eugenio Spritzer. Assuming for the sake of argument that Spritzer wasn't directly involved in the homicides, what the hell *was* he up to? Emil knew he'd heard Spritzer's half-cocky, half-simpering voice on the phone hoping that Sarah "stayed happy." That call, that remark, had apparently been inspired by the *Trib*'s notice that Corky was relying on Emil in the murder investigation.

But Spritzer was certainly no newcomer to Stearns County. Didn't he know—hadn't he heard?—that such a comment was absolutely guaranteed to get Emil's Dutch up? Get old and a little idle, be surprised how much

Dutch you've stored away. So why would Spritzer have made that call, and the other calls?

Then Emil perceived a fallacy in his own approach. He was looking for logic. He was expecting to discover a rational pattern. But there was at least one maniac running around loose in Stearns County. Maniacs aren't too predictable, when you come right down to it.

"I've gotta see Bishop Bundeswehr," Emil murmured to himself.

"What?" asked Riley, at the wheel.

"Said it's about time for me to go to church."

The last several miles into St. Cloud proved tough going, but beautiful too. It was dark now and the headlights of the van fashioned swirling twin tunnels of soft light, gorgeous and shimmering, against curtains of snow, living walls of the world come down to shroud the land in peace.

"What would you have done if you'd been out in weather like this in the old days?" Riley asked.

"Prayed," Emil said. "There may be an advantage or two in this new-fangled internal combustion engine."

The St. Cloud plows were out and working. Riley made it to the north side with no trouble and dropped Emil at his house. Declining an invitation to come in for supper, he drove off. Sarah met Emil at the door, but instead of scolding him for not having the good sense to come in out of a blizzard, she rushed him to the TV.

"The evening news on KSTP is just starting. The anchorman mentioned Stearns County and the murders! Do you think Corky'll be on?"

If he memorized his speech, Emil thought. "Let's watch and see."

Emil shook off snow in the hallway, pulled off his boots, hung up his coat, and walked over to his rocking chair.

The newscast began with the day's big story.

"A blizzard is sweeping into the Upper Northwest tonight . . . " the reporter began. There followed the usual assortment of storm shots, cars barely visible beneath drifts, pedestrians being blown down Minneapolis streets, and an overturned semi-trailer on some highway somewhere. "I think they're using film from the '51 blizzard this time," Emil said. "I remember that pedestrian with the white fur coat and heart-shaped goggles."

The big moment came at the end of the telecast. "Vicious double murder in Stearns County . . . "

And there was Sheriff Corky Withers on the screen, with the courthouse dome in the background. Corky ought not to have worried. He looked good, did well, showing only the faintest trace of nervousness, which, considering his youth and earnest demeanor, turned out to be an advantage. It was what Corky said that troubled Emil.

" . . . yes, we here in Stearns County feel that the case is solved. The alleged perpetrator, Felix Miggs, originally arrested on suspicion, has now been formally charged with two counts of homicide in the first degree. He'll be taking a polygraph test today, at his own request."

Emil realized the lie-detector test was already history. He would have to call Corky and see how it had turned out.

"The District Attorney hopes to bring the case to trial by early February."

"Corky looked good," said Sarah, pleased, as the weatherman came on to tell everybody that the storm was veering toward the northeast, across the Great Lakes.

Corky looked very good, but he's wrong, Emil thought.

After dinner, Emil paged through the new issue of *Field and Stream,* which had come in the mail. Hell, he ought to go up to Lake Superior for smelt this spring. Hadn't done that for four, no five years. Sarah was wrapping a stack of romantic novels, a gift for Dory, who doted on them. Her favorite author was Vanessa Royall.

"Dory told me she might try writing a romance herself," Sarah said. "Everybody seems to be doing it."

"How is her spelling?" said Emil, thinking of the letter he'd received. "I've got something here I'd like you to take a look at."

He pulled it out and showed it to his wife, who read it with puzzled fascination. "Where did you get this, Emil?"

"Came in the mail the other morning."

"You didn't tell me."

"Didn't want to disturb you. You were on the phone. But I've a question for you now. Let's just say Father Creedmore did kill Mrs. Miggs and her boy."

"Oh, Emil, I find that so hard to believe."

"For the sake of argument, all right? 'Aynimous' here says he and his wife know the killer pretty well. Now, in your various comings and goings, Rosary Society, sodality, ladies' auxiliary, you ever see a married couple in Father Creedmore's company?"

"Let me think. Mostly he's with Mr. Spritzer, the one from Right-to-Life."

"Think hard."

"Let me see, a married couple. Oh! Twice at Holy Spirit's Bingo Bazaar, I saw him with Gregor and Ilsa Kufelski. Does that mean anything?"

Dink Kufelski! Emil leaned sharply backward in his chair. Dink, owner of the Dippi-Freez. Who had asked, just yesterday, how the investigation was going.

"May mean something, may not," he told Sarah. No sense getting her all excited.

The phone rang. Sarah answered. It was Corky, and he wanted to talk to Emil.

"Saw you on the tube," Emil began, "you did real well. Don't agree with what you said, though."

Corky's video success seemed not to have touched him.

"Where've you been?" he asked. It came just short of a demand.

"Oh, driving around."

"Emil, you went to Minneapolis, didn't you? Well, forget that. It's a dry hole. We've got problems."

"Oh?" Emil said.

"After I was on TV, Flinch Miggs took the polygraph test. And then his kid, Josh, came over from the hospital and took the test too. Their lawyer, Stein, came around and agreed to it."

"Corky, you don't sound happy."

"Emil, they both passed. With flying colors. I know the polygraph is not admissible evidence anyway, but—"

"Corky, I told you who the murderer is, and when you find out what I saw in Minneapolis today—"

"Wait. There's a catch to the Miggs' tests. They're completely invalid."

"What? I thought you said—"

"No, listen. When the boy was taken back to the hospital, one of the nurses noticed blood on his right middle finger. He gave her some grief . . . "

Emil could imagine mean-mouthed little Josh giving grief.

" . . . but she checked it anyway. Something had been inserted under his fingernail."

"That would hurt."

"That's the point. The kid bragged that he'd stuck a pin under his nail during the polygraph test, so he'd be thinking of pain during all the questions. Guilt—if any—would be the last thing on his mind. And, Emil?"

"I'm right here."

"When I heard about that, I checked Flinch's hands. I went back in the cell myself. He had a bloody fingertip and a blue nail too. That shows they were *both* in on the murder but meanwhile lawyer Stein is calling for a complete and immediate dismissal of the charges. What do you think?"

"I thought Flinch was worth arresting on suspicion. But now I'm sure he didn't do it. Neither did his kid. Let 'em go. Don't make them earn life sentences out of their own stupidity."

"But, Emil, I said on TV—"

"Forget that."

"Who do you think did it?" Corky demanded.

"You know damn well who I think did it."

"That'll never wash. Not in this county. We can't go with that."

Emil was just about to tell Corky of the anonymous letter, but he decided against it, for the time being. He wanted to talk to Dink Kufelski first.

"You'll be getting a call from Father Rogers at the Chancery," Corky said.

"You seem to know an awful lot of things."

"Emil, let me cut the nut. I've been in touch with the Chancery, and they've been in touch with me. There's been an awful lot of underground chatter, a lot of rumors, going around, and the Chancery thinks it's about time to lay that stuff to rest. It's not good for the county to have vicious stories about Father Creedmore circulating in every store, in every bar and grill."

"That has plenty to do with Rogers and Bundeswehr, dammit. Do you realize that two murders have occurred? And that the Chancery's covering up for Creedmore?"

"Flinch Miggs is the murderer, Emil," said Corky wearily. "I've got him right here in jail."

It was no use. "Call me tomorrow, if you want to," Emil said. He hung up. "Special deputy," he humphed.

He had a brandy at the kitchen table, and Sarah told him what she had decided upon for Christmas Day dinner: Turkey with wild rice stuffing, boiled yams—"Since they're sweet enough by themselves and people our age don't need any more sugar"—lettuce, salad, and cherry pie.

"Good enough for me," said Emil. "Sounds familiar, though. No, wait, I think we had ham instead of turkey ten, eleven years ago."

"Oh, you! You can cook the dinner if you want to, and then see where we'd be!"

"I can? Okay, let's see. Bunch of Tom and Jerries. Chili, sure, that'd be pretty good."

"Huh! You repeat all day when you have chili."

"I do not. I have a cast-iron stomach. Always have."

The phone rang again. Sarah answered it. "Hello? Hello?"

"Nobody there," she said, hanging up.

"Somebody's there, all right," contradicted Emil, thinking of Eugenio Spritzer.

The phone rang again. "I'll get it this time," Emil said. "Hey," he growled, lifting the receiver, "you want to tell me something, you get over here like a man and do it! What? Oh. Oh, Father Rogers! No, sorry. I thought you were somebody else." He listened a bit, said "sure," and hung up.

"Father Rogers is on his way over to pick me up," he told Sarah. "I'm going to have a talk with the bishop."

14

F or once, at least, the weatherman had been right. By the time Father Rogers pulled up in front of Whippletree's house, proudly piloting that big Imperial, the storm was slackening a little. Dipping his cane into a drift, Emil reckoned that maybe a foot had fallen since late afternoon. A foot was practically nothing. Bush league stuff.

"How you doin', Father?" asked Emil, getting into the car.

"How are *you* doing?" The way he asked it made Emil feel that maybe he wasn't doing too well.

"How do you like this snow?" Emil asked.

"Right on time for Christmas."

That just about exhausted the weather as a topic of conversation. Father Rogers drove south, swung onto Ring Road past the Cathedral, and toward the Mississippi River.

"We'll have a small party after midnight Mass. His Excellency always insists upon it. Father Creedmore, by the way, is His Excellency's choice to give the homily at midnight Mass."

This information was casually stated. *Very* casually stated. Since time immemorial, Bishop Bundeswehr himself had given the homily. Emil quit talking and appreciated the interior of the Chrysler—window curtains, jump seats, telephone, and a small refrigerator-and-bar. He wondered if Bundeswehr could still handle Tom and Jerries. They were pretty high in cholesterol. Bundeswehr was seventy-three, two years older than Emil.

Father Rogers stopped in front of the mansion, a Victorian pile of brick near the Mississippi, built by some forgotten lumber baron during the first flush frontier days. This was the Historic Homes section of town; old Bundeswehr enjoyed living here.

Emil was surprised when His Excellency greeted him at the door, smiling, smiling. Bundeswehr, in public, was almost always smiling, which pushed upward his soft, chubby cheeks, the better to distract from the constant movement of his shrewd little eyes. Those eyes didn't miss much.

Bundeswehr was wearing a simple black cassock—no breast cross, no beanie—as if he had decided that Emil could best be approached with the common touch. He commanded a finely tuned, dazzlingly orchestrated symphony of attitudes and postures, guises and poses, and only those who had known or observed him closely for decades could tell whether the flicker of an eyebrow signaled amusement or terminal disapprobation. Probably the young Wilhelm Bundeswehr had flickered his eyebrows, tilted his head, lifted his hand exactly as he did now, but way back then no one had reason to read significance into a young cleric's tics and quivers. Things were different now.

Smiling, Bundeswehr offered his hand. Emil shook it. He offered his ring. Emil bent to it.

"Father Rogers, take Emil's coat, please. And bring us some tea. Emil, let's go into the parlor, shall we?"

Bundeswehr's parlor was sober, ornate, and flamboyant, this last touch accomplished by thick, red-velvet draperies, so rich they glowed dully in lamplight. Bundeswehr gestured toward the windows, a slow, easy movement of his hand. "Red," he said, with a deep gurgle meant to sound like self-deprecating laughter. "It's as close as I'll ever get to cardinal."

They sat down at opposite ends of a low couch and each old man made the inevitable physical evaluation of the other. Bundeswehr had put on a little more weight, Emil observed, a burden he didn't need. Ecclesiastics tended to pack on the fat in their thirties and forties, hold on in their fifties, and then lose the excess either by will-power or illness in their sixties. If they lived into their seventies, they often began to look ascetic. Bundeswehr, however, looked fat and healthy. A delicate mesh of purple veins was visible beneath the skin of his cheeks and nose, much like the skin of an old woman surfeited too often by too much strudel and cream, but Emil had to admit that His Excellency looked pretty fit for a man of seventy-three.

Father Rogers brought in a tray with teapot, cream, and sugar. He poured two cups and asked how they wanted it.

"Straight," said Emil.

"Same for me, thank you, Father," said the bishop, not happily.

Father Rogers withdrew. Emil and Bundeswehr sipped tea. Now we get down to business, Emil thought. He had been summoned here and he was going to wait for the Bishop to make his pitch.

"Well, Emil," said the bishop now, setting his teacup down on the coffee table, "how about a cigar?"

"Fine, thanks."

"Father Rogers? Father Rogers, bring in the humidor, would you?"

The balding priest hustled in immediately. He had to have been hovering just outside the door. Emil was reminded of Eugenio Spritzer, lurking outside Father Creedmore's study. He wondered where the bishop's tape recorder was.

"Havana," said the bishop proudly, as Emil selected a rich brown panatela from the mahogany humidor. The bishop did likewise. Father Rogers fired them up with pine tapers and withdrew.

The cigar was very good, mild and rich in taste, but Emil would have preferred a chaw of Svobriskie. Good old Bundeswehr, he was thinking.

"I recall a time," the bishop began, invoking anecdote and parable, "when I read about a situation pretty much like the one we have now."

Emil did not miss the manner in which "we" had been emphasized.

"Yes, yes, very much like our current problem. Ever read Thucydides, Emil?"

"Ah—no." Emil always hated this kind of thing.

"No matter. The point is what's important. And the point is that in the famous debate between Thucydides and St. Augustine we have the key to our problem here in Stearns County."

Emil waited. He had heard of St. Augustine any number of times. Bundeswehr puffed on his cigar.

"Emil, Thucydides was a promulgator, a fierce promulgator of the doctrine of the greater good. You know what I mean?"

"Not in so many words."

"Thucydides believed the community was manifest, was most important. He wasn't all that excited about the rights of the individual."

"And St. Augustine was?"

"He was. He most definitely was. And in their big debate, the one in Carthage, Augustine decimated the other guy. That's what's important to us here." Bundeswehr leaned forward, flicked a long length of white ash into an ashtray, sat back again. He gave Emil a fervent, black-eyed glare.

"Emil, we have got to protect the individual in this current case, and he is Father Peter Creedmore."

Now that business was finally imminent, Emil didn't see any point in pussyfooting around. Details he could handle. Carthage and all that other stuff made him uneasy.

"I've got reason to believe Father Creedmore killed Mrs. Miggs and her son," he told His Excellency.

"Couldn't be."

"He was at the scene just before the crime occurred."

"He admits it. *Before* the crime occurred. He was on his way to a sick call."

"It wasn't a call. Mrs. Heiderscheidt never called him."

Momentarily, Bundeswehr looked flustered. "Doesn't matter," he told Emil. "Accident of circumstances. He had no motive. That's what you lawmen have to look for. A motive."

Emil told him about the hollering match between Creedmore and Trixie outside the confessional, about the abortion, and about Dr. Bradley's film showing Father Creedmore attacking a woman.

"Bishop, your boy is sick," Emil told him. "I know he was a patient up at St. Concepta's Home for a time, and I wonder just where you had him treated from 1970 to 1975, down there in Washington, D.C."

Bundeswehr's head rocked back a little, which caused him to lose a couple of chins temporarily.

"I doubt he was teaching Sacred Theology at Catholic University," Emil went on. "It would be easy to check, though."

"Yes," grunted Bundeswehr, getting his chins back by lowering his jaw to his chest. "But he didn't *kill* anybody!"

"How do you know?"

"How could he? He's a man of God."

"So was Matthew Koster."

"That was different. Koster was a Protestant. Emil, you solved the Koster case. That's all well and good. But now since there's another crime, you think a churchman is guilty again. It's not the same. Father Creedmore is under tremendous strain, *tremendous* strain. It's my duty to protect him, and it's your responsibility to let him alone. He might snap."

"It's my responsibility to find the killer, Bishop."

Bundeswehr took some rapid, shallow puffs. He was no longer enjoying the Havana. "Take it from me, Emil, Peter Creedmore is incapable of killing."

"If he's capable of attacking a woman from behind, with a camera running, why wouldn't he be capable of shooting somebody?"

The bishop glowered. "All right, Emil. But why shoot the boys? I mean, he didn't, nor did he shoot Mrs. Miggs. But, even if granted that he shot the woman, why the boys?"

Emil took the cigar out of his mouth and rested it in the V between index and middle fingers. "Rage. Creedmore's a sick man."

"Others will testify to this?"

Emil thought of the anonymous letter in his coat pocket.

"I think so," he said.

"Emil, the Church—"

"Bishop, the law—"

Bundeswehr discarded some chins and looked at Emil over the bridge of his delicately curved nose. "All right, Emil," he said, "What do you want?"

"What do I want?"

"Yes. What do you need in order to leave Father Creedmore alone? His is a sad story. I don't think he killed anybody. I'm going to stand by him."

"How sad is his story?"

Bundeswehr thought something over for a long moment.

"All right," he said, "but what I tell you remains between us."

Emil nodded. His cigar was dead. He put it in the ashtray. Bundeswehr's was dead too, but he relit it with a match. "It was clear from the time Father Creedmore was ordained," he told Emil, "that something was a little different about him. You know much about seminaries?"

"Nope."

"Well, you have to remember that, by the time they're ordained, these young men have been cooped up for a long time, under the tremendous tension not only of study but also of having to take vows that will bind them for life. Mostly, they've had little experience of the world. A lot of giggling and horseplay goes on. But that's all right. It's a way to let off steam. Then, after ordination, there is a period characterized by euphoria. That's fine too."

The bishop paused and puffed.

"So?" Emil said.

"Father Creedmore was a different kind of duck. He was dour and driven in seminary, and he didn't change any after ordination. In fact, he got worse."

"So you sent him up to St. Concepta's?"

"Yes."

"Any particular reason?"

"He had a breakdown. I recognized him as a nervous type, of course, and I tried to get him out a little, get him into the lighter activities of the diocese. I made him youth chaplain. He was in charge of setting up softball, basketball, picnics in the summer. Stuff like that."

"What happened?"

"After three weeks, attendance was off sixty-two percent. Sixty-two percent! Before every event, he'd take all the kids over to the cathedral and have them say the rosary. I had to appoint a new youth chaplain. Kids should pray, but they ought to get to play, too. Pete didn't understand that."

"He must have been upset when you gave another priest the job?"

"I'm sure he was. He felt unworthy. He's always felt unworthy, and he tries too hard to compensate for it. But, no, the actual breakdown occurred at a meeting of the Rosary Society. By the way, my congratulations to your wife on her election."

"Thanks, I'll pass it along. She's very pleased."

"Father Creedmore got into a dispute with the Rosary Society's officers," the bishop said. "Tanys Voorde was head of it then, as I recall. Creedmore shouldn't have had to do anything but lead the opening prayer, stick around and smile a little, and then get on out. That's what the chaplains had always done, and that's what Tanys and her friends expected Father Creedmore to do. But he didn't. He wanted to run the show. Now, Emil, if you know Tanys Voorde, you know we are dealing with—you'll forgive the expression—a tough broad."

Emil had to agree. The only woman in town meaner than Tanys was probably Florence Hockapuk, Sarah's rival.

"In any event, the Rosary Society voted to donate the proceeds of its annual clothing sale to the orphanage. Creedmore said no."

"Why did he say no?" Emil asked. "What charity did he want?"

Bundeswehr looked embarrassed. "All I know is what Mrs. Voorde said, which was that Father Creedmore believed God willed the suffering of those who were abandoned—"

"What?" growled Emil.

"—and giving money to them was like spitting in God's eye. Father Creedmore doesn't remember saying anything like that."

"I hope not. That was his breakdown?"

"Coming up. Tanys said something critical to him, he slapped her face, the other women of the Rosary Society started yelling. Father Creedmore fled. The phone calls went back and forth. Emil, I earned my pay that day! Some kids found Father later in the park, on his knees, praying to the statue of James J. Hill. We had him up at St. Concepta's next day, and later on sent him to D.C. He improved a lot there. Really. He even did some teaching."

"And now he's pastor at St. Hrothgar's in Silverton. I

know it's not a big parish, but Father obviously takes his responsibilities very seriously. You sure he's up to the pressure?"

"Emil, I agonized over that one, I tell you. But his doctors said he was ready for it, and Father thought so too. Can't you see my position? I had to give him a chance, give him a shot at making a comeback, so to speak. He needs support."

"Well, I doubt he's getting the best support there is from this guy, Spritzer."

Bishop Bundeswehr's small eyes narrowed, almost disappeared in the fatty folds of his face. "I know they work together on Life Saviors—" he began.

"I think they're a lot closer than that. I've been told Spritzer is out there at the rectory all the time."

"Is that so?" said the bishop, noncommitally. "Is that so? I'll check into it. You know how it is, Emil. The head man doesn't know everything because there are things his subordinates keep from him. For his own good, of course."

"And for their own reasons," said Emil. "I was sheriff, remember? I had quite a bunch of deputies."

"Well, Emil, let me check up on this Spritzer thing, all right? But, I assure you again, Father Creedmore is coming along fine."

Talking about it further wouldn't get either of them anywhere, so Emil pulled out the anonymous letter and handed it to Bundeswehr. The bishop's eyebrows arched higher and higher as he read it.

"Mailed to you privately?" he asked, handing it back.

"Yup."

"An illiterate."

"I'm not so sure. The writer is afraid for his wife. That's obvious. And he thinks Father Creedmore is dangerous."

"Doesn't say anything about Father Creedmore in there."

"Not by name. But he says I'm on the right track. And the way talk goes in this county, a lot of people know that I think Creedmore's the killer."

"Emil, I just can't accept it. I can't remove him in the face of those vicious stories. I have to hold firm. A man's career is at stake."

The two old men sat there, at sharp odds but not angry, not yet.

"You and I are the old guard, Emil. We can't let this blow up. We know how things go. No dirty linen in public, right?"

"I don't like dirty linen any better than you do, and I'll do everything I can. But I am a special deputy and I have a job to do. How about this? You give the go-ahead for Father Creedmore to take a polygraph test, and in return I guarantee nobody will find out about it."

"Felix Miggs and his son took the polygraph and the whole county knows it already."

"I'll have it done by my friend Jiggsy Potoff from the Bureau of Criminal Apprehension. If you think your priest is innocent, put him to the test. An act of faith, you might say."

Bundeswehr hesitated.

"Well, do you believe in the guy or not?" Whippletree prodded.

"All right." The bishop bowed his head gravely, and achieved six chins. He looked tired.

"Emil," he said a bit later, offering his ring after seeing the old sheriff to the door, "what are we doing? This should be our happy old age, time to relax and reap the benefits of years well-spent. Instead, here we are, blundering around in God knows what."

Whippletree bent his lips to the ring, but he resisted the nostalgia and the sentiment. Bundeswehr wasn't "blundering around" at all, and Emil damn well knew it.

"You'd rather sit by the fire, then, is that it?" he asked

his host. Outside, Father Rogers was gunning the Imperial, warming it up to drive Emil back home. "You'd like to sit by the fire and rock and fret in your old age, am I right?"

Old Bundeswehr was half-a-head shorter than Emil, but his usual stance was regal, and he assumed it now. "Hell no," he declared.

"Amen," said Emil.

15

Next morning, Emil was awake early and raring to go. He'd arranged for Jiggsy Potoff of the BCA to drive up from The Cities and administer the polygraph to Father Creedmore. The test was to be conducted in a room at the Holiday Inn. All hush-hush. Before the test, Emil would have time to stop by the Dippi-Freeze and talk to Dink Kufelski, "aynimous" himself.

But, early as Emil was up, and raring as he felt, Corky was ahead of him. Emil was still in the kitchen in his bathrobe when Corky knocked and entered, crisp and fresh, polished and pressed and lemon-limey. Worried as hell.

"Emil, Bawlie Wepner's dead," he said.

Sarah, busy frying bacon at the stove, whirled around. "Another killing?" She faltered.

"Naw, he wasn't murdered," sighed Corky, sagging into a chair, joining Emil at the kitchen table. He had brought the *Trib* in from the porch and he shoved it across the bright yellow-and-white-checked tablecloth. "Doc Divot says he froze to death."

"The heat was on in his house when we left him," Emil blurted. He felt sad, somehow responsible. He felt angry, too, at the waste Bawlie's life had been. HERE LIES PAUL E. WEPNER, VICTIM OF THE SYNDROME.

"*You* were at Bawlie's house?" cried Corky. "You and who else? *When?*

Emil regretted his outburst. "Yes," he answered. "Bawlie'd had a lot to drink. Riley and Nubs and I got him bedded down in his house. Piled on plenty of blankets. And I swear the heat was *on*."

"Oh, dear," mourned Sarah, gingerly removing strips of lean bacon from the sizzling pan. "Corky, have you had breakfast?"

"Yes, ma'am. I'll take some coffee, though, if you don't mind." He turned back to Emil. "Bawlie didn't die in his house," he said. "Ron Youngdahl, who works the county snowplow out there, found Bawlie's body in the ditch midway between his place and Silverton. Just before six this morning. Couple of hours ago. His Dough-Rite truck had gotten stuck in a drift. Bawlie was apparently trying to get to Silverton on foot. Probably to get more booze. Damn shame. Too bad. You said he'd been drinking heavily?"

Sarah served bacon and biscuits, poured coffee for the men. Emil concentrated on buttering a biscuit. He didn't want to reveal by word or expression that he doubted Corky's explanation. Bawlie hadn't left his house in order to get more liquor. He'd set out for Silverton to make a phone call!

—Emuhl, the murd—I knowgh—

Bawlie had come to sometime during the night, and had decided that his information couldn't wait until morning. But why hadn't he called from his house? There was no need to go to Silverton.

Or was there? Nubs Tufo didn't have a phone, he didn't believe in them, and the Miggs house was locked and sealed.

Something must have gone wrong with Bawlie's phone. Maybe the blizzard had knocked down the lines. It happened.

Emil left his breakfast, got up, and went to the phone.

"What do you want, dear?" asked Sarah, who had just sat down at the table.

"Ah . . . I just had an impulse to check with the Highway Department," Emil fibbed. "Hugh and Dory'll be getting an early start tomorrow, and I want to make sure everything is clear from here to Iowa."

He riffled through the directory, found Wepner's number, and dialed. Nothing happened, no clicks of connections being made, no ringing phone, only a thin electric howl stretching from Emil's ear to the fields of infinity and abyss.

"Looking good," he said cheerfully, sitting down at the table again, "all roads clear and no new snow expected."

He picked up a strip of bacon and began crunching it—still had all his teeth except two molars on the lower right—but he hardly tasted the meat. His mind was on Bawlie's house, Bawlie's phone, and a man who seemed to know a lot about communications devices. Roy Riley. Yesterday, while Emil and Nubs had been settling Bawlie on the couch, Roy Riley, searching for blankets, might have had the opportunity to do something to the telephone. Emil liked the reporter, enjoyed his youth and his wit. But Riley *had* admitted to a sexual relationship with Trixie Miggs. There *was* a connection.

Corky sipped coffee, looking vaguely woeful, and Sarah paged through the *Morning Tribune*.

"Here's my interview!" she cried happily, scanning the article and then reading it slowly. Emil leaned over to note the headline. SARAH WHIPPLETREE NEW ROSARY SOCIETY PREZ.

"Oh, that Roy Riley is really a good writer, don't you think?"

Corky Withers looked pained.

"Anything in the paper about the Miggs case?" Emil asked dryly.

"No," answered Corky, but that fact, which yesterday had seemed almost a triumph, did not lift the young sheriff's spirits today.

"You looked good on KSTP-TV," Sarah told him.

Corky winced. "I wonder how I'll look next time," he moaned. "They want to talk to me again. They're going to make me look like an ass—sorry, Mrs. Whippletree—for sure."

"Corky, why?"

"Because of what I told them yesterday. That Flinch Miggs was the perpetrator and the case was all wrapped up."

"Well," said Emil, as gently as he could, "you shouldn't have told them that to begin with. Booking Flinch on suspicion was one thing, but Father Creedmore is the prime suspect. You've got to deal with that fact, sooner or later, or your career as sheriff won't be worth much."

"My career as *anything*," pronounced Corky bleakly. "KSTP is going to want to know why, if Flinch Miggs was the killer yesterday, he's out scot-free today."

"Flinch has been released?" Emil exclaimed. Maybe things were getting sane around town after all.

"It had to be done. Not only did he pass, without a glitch, a *second* lie detector test—this was after the one where he stuck a pin under his fingernail—a bunch of guys from out in the country came in and gave him an alibi as to his whereabouts on the murder night."

"A bunch of guys?"

"Yeah. They were afraid to come forward earlier, but I put Deputy Gosch to work on it. He started with Ebenscheider at Crossroad Auto Supply, where Flinch fueled his pickup truck. Gosch managed to trace Flinch's itinerary for the whole murder night. Jamie is a better detail man than I figured."

Emil took a reading and realized that Corky was envious of his deputy.

"Anyway," said Corky disconsolately, "Barney Elderkopf, who runs the Quail and Tail bar in Pearl Lake, swears that Flinch was there drinking with him from a little after two until five in the morning. Barney's passed a polygraph on that himself. Flinch's lawyer, Stein, threatened to sue the county for false arrest if his client wasn't released. The Board of Commissioners caved in. So we haven't got a suspect at all, now. What'll I tell the TV guys today?"

"Tell them about Father Peter Creedmore."

"Oh, Emil, this is all so sad," commented Sarah.

"I know it," he said grimly. "What about the boy?" he asked Corky. "What about Josh?"

"He's out of the hospital, with his father."

"Wonderful."

"Emil . . ." Corky faltered, not meeting the older man's eyes. "Emil, what if Father Creedmore flunks that lie detector test this morning?"

What the hell? thought Whippletree. Bundeswehr had insisted the test be hush-hush. How did Corky know about it? Why? Emil had the feeling he was being set up for a fall. Again. "How did you find out about that?" he demanded.

Corky evaded Emil's question. "The Board of Commissioner's did authorize funds for a radio scrambler, though," he said. "Roy Riley won't be up our—sorry, Mrs. Whippletree—down our necks every minute. It'll be months before we actually have the scrambler though," Corky admitted ruefully. "Doesn't do me much good right now. Emil, can I be present for Father's polygraph test? I understand you're in charge."

"Who told you that?"

"Well, I don't want to say."

"Father Rogers?"

Corky blushed, but didn't bother to try a lie.

"Why don't you just send over Jamie Gosch, sort of as an observer?" Emil suggested, rattling Corky's cage a bit. "Have him meet me over at the motel."

Sheriff Withers was startled.

"I'm sure Corky can handle it," said Sarah encouragingly. "More coffee?"

The lawmen declined. Emil told Corky to meet him at the Holiday Inn and went upstairs to get dressed.

A few minutes later he was in his car, heading west on busy Division Street. Everybody and his brother was out shopping already. St. Cloud merchants would count plenty of bills and coins today.

Which is exactly what Gregor "Dink" Kufelski was doing when Emil entered the Dippi-Freeze via the back door, where the manager's office was located. Up front, a teenage boy in white apron and peaked white cap was busy preparing the daily batch of Dippi-Freeze by pouring milk, sugar, and a "secret powder" into a refrigerated blending machine, and Ilsa, Dink's wife, labored over ten-gallon vats of chili, bratwurst, and enough sauerkraut to put Axel Vogel in hog heaven. Dink glanced up from counting money, raised a hand, motioned Emil to a chair, and went on counting.

"Damn it," he said, after a minute, "lost my count." He looked up at Emil. He looked nervous. "Got to get the change money right or the help'll steal me blind," he said with a nervous smile.

"I guess I came at the wrong time."

"No, Emil. No, of course not. Not at all."

Emil looked at Kufelski and Dink stared back. But not for long.

"Okay, Emil. I apologize for sending you an anonymous letter. It was a dumb kid thing to do."

"Not necessarily. You're not the first guy in history who didn't want to get mixed up in a murder case."

"Shhhhh! Ilsa!" cried Dink, alarmed. "She doesn't know."

"Sorry."

"How'd you find out it was me who sent the letter?"

"You and Ilsa have been seen around with Father Creedmore. Your letter indicates that you know him pretty well. Can't hide the facts with a faked case of bad typing. Why'd you do that, anyway?"

"Like you said, I didn't want to get involved. I figured

I'd tell you what I had to say, because I think it's important."

"Why didn't you send the note to Corky? After all, he's sheriff."

"Corky? Shit." Dink glanced through the doorway and into the kitchen, where his wife was mixing up a bowl of tangy "special" sauce to go with the bratwurst. "I wouldn't put it past Creedmore to kill," he told Emil.

"Why do you think that?"

"Known him a long time. Who knows how well? Depends on which one of him he's showing that day."

Emil frowned. Dink had a point. Emil pulled Dink's letter out of his pocket. "Couple of questions," he said.

"Shoot."

"Here you say Creedmore knows the layout of your house, and that you're afraid for Ilsa if she's there alone?"

"Sure am. It started on Thanksgiving. We had Father over for dinner. I know him from back at Pater Noster. We had some classes together in prep school there. I never went on to college, though. On account of lack of money. On account of lack of ambition, more likely." Dink shrugged. He was a commonsense kind of guy, generally happy with himself and the Dippi-Freeze franchise. "Anyway, he always struck me like he needed a friend, so when he comes back here after that long stint of teaching in Washington D.C., I started inviting him to the house now and then, even though he made Ilsa nervous."

"Why was that?"

"I'm not sure."

"Anyway, on Thanksgiving?"

"Sure. We were having a couple of beers before dinner, Father Pete and Ilsa and me, and he sort of changed. He can be very charming. He can charm the serpents right down from the trees, like they used to say at Pater Noster. But we had us some beers and he starts to get, well, a little mean."

"In what way?"

"Well, Ilsa and me, we got married kind of late. Ilsa's a Stearns County farm girl, but she's had a hard life. Real hard. She doesn't want kids, and I accept that."

"But Father Creedmore—?"

"You got it, Emil. He had him a couple of beers and then jumped on her back about not having kids."

"He's one of the Life Saviors."

"They ought to butt out of other people's business, if you ask me. I never in a million years believed Father Pete would pull that kind of shit in my house. On Thanksgiving. *While drinking my beer!*"

"How did Ilsa handle it?"

"Like she handles me when her dander's up. She told him off, reamed him up one side and down the other. Truth to tell, I was sort of proud of her."

The teenager stuck his head in the doorway. "Mr. Kufelski, we're out of strawberry syrup."

"Okay. I'll put some more on order. Push chocolate and vanilla today."

"Dink, would you ever consider telling any of this in, say, a court?"

The Dippi-Freez proprietor looked as if he'd been pole-axed.

"Court? A trial? Emil, *no way.*" Dink Kufelski was pleading. "I never would have sent you the letter if I'd thought it would come to that."

Emil handed him the typed page and the envelope too. Dink ripped them into tiny tatters, sighing with relief.

"Emil, I knew I could count on you," he said.

"In that letter, you mentioned something about a hand-writing sample?"

"Yeah." Dink nodded. "Whenever we took Father Pete along with us to Bingo, or a picnic, or whatever, he'd always send a nice little thank-you note. But it struck me as funny, because every note was, like, in a different handwriting. Oh, it was him, all right, he had written it, but it was . . . different. So I saw in this magazine one time an ad to get your handwriting analyzed. 'I'll play a good trick on Father Pete,' I thought. So I pieced some of his thank-you notes together and mailed them in."

"Father didn't think much of the trick?"

"Hell, I was scared to tell him the results. I was scared *of* the results. The handwriting guy wrote back and said something like, 'you know analysis and you're trying to put one over, because the sample you sent is the handwriting of a person who is mentally ill.' Emil, I swear it's true."

"I believe you. But you wouldn't testify to this?"

"Emil, I have to live in Stearns County. This is where I do my business. Thanks for giving me the letter back, and all, but, really, I think I've done my part."

"You have helped," the old sheriff told Dink. "Let me ask you one more question, if you don't mind?"

Dink glanced at his watch. "Ilsa, don't boil the brats too long, okay?" he called. "They lose their juice."

There was a short silence, marred only by furious bubbling in the bratwurst pot, and then Ilsa Kufelski barged into the room. "Boil them yourself," she said, "if you're the only one who can—oh, hi, Emil!"

"Ilsa," said Emil, leaning on his cane a little and getting to his feet gallantly.

"Look, Dink, this is a gentleman."

"You're looking good, Ilsa."

Ilsa not only looked good, she looked really good. One of Stearns County's lush, strong blondes, her body had been tempered young by throwing bales of hay around. There weren't too many people who were going to tell her what to think or do, or how to live.

"What can we do for you, Emil?" she asked. "Want some lunch?"

Dink looked pained. He had not wanted his wife in on this.

"What's with you?" Ilsa demanded of her husband. "You sick, or something?"

"I'm here on a little business," Emil interjected, saving old Dink from further cross-examination. "It's about Father Peter Creedmore."

"That jerk!" said Ilsa.

"I only have one more question to ask," Emil said, "and it's this. During the time you've known Father Creedmore, what is the strangest thing you can recall?"

"Well, Thanksgiving, like I told you," Dink said. "Right, honey?"

"No," Ilsa disagreed, "there was something weirder. Dink, remember last summer at that picnic on Sportsman's Island? Everybody was having a good time, but there was Father Pete practically crying in his beer? Maybe you didn't hear him, but he said something that seemed, to me anyway, the craziest thing I'd ever heard in my life! That's why I remembered it, it was so scary. It sounded—what do they call it—sacrilegious? *Nothing surpasses never having been born.'* That's what he said."

"Tell me," Emil asked her, "are you afraid of Peter Creedmore?"

Ilsa thought it over. "Broad daylight," she said, "one on one, no. Dark night, him with a gun, yes."

"So you think Father Pete is capable of killing?" Emil pressed.

Ilsa didn't hesitate. "Sure," she said. "Isn't it obvious? I'm just a Stearns County farm girl, but even I can see that."

16

The Lincoln sped across the Holiday Inn parking lot,
loose crosslink of tire chain banging inside a fender.
Jiggsy Potoff, Sheriff Corky Withers, and Emil were
standing around the exit door at the rear of the Holiday
Inn, waiting.

"Looks like Spritzer's bringing Father Creedmore for
the test," Emil said. "I'd better duck out of sight. Seeing
me is sure to upset him, and we want the test to be as
straight as possible."

"Like I told you," said Potoff, "the polygraph is never
foolproof, but the metabolism of the average person does
fluctuate when he lies, and that's what the machine mea-
sures. Of course, when you're testing pathological sub-
jects, you might not get any variations at all. Their inner
reality is so strong, so warped, that truth and falsehood
cease to have any meaning."

"Emil, let's go get a cup of coffee and leave this to Mr.
Potoff," Corky suggested.

"You go ahead. I'll just wait in my car."

Emil slid into his Chevy, ducked down low. Corky
walked off around the corner of the Holiday Inn and out
of sight. Spritzer's big car made a sharp left and headed
toward Potoff, who waved. Spritzer parked a few spaces
from Emil's car.

The plan called for Potoff to take Father Creedmore
upstairs to a second-floor room, where the polygraph machine had been set up. Everything was hush-hush. Emil
was keeping his bargain of secrecy with Bishop Bundeswehr.

From under the brim of his favorite felt hat, pulled down low over his eyes, he saw Father Creedmore and Spritzer emerge from the Lincoln. Creedmore looked as if he'd aged ten years during the last couple of days, the harsh gray of his Brillo-pad hair distinctly whiter. In spite of his barrel-chested heft, the priest seemed fragile, bent. He walked unsteadily, turning his thick head from left to right, as if trying to get up the nerve to look over his shoulder and see who was on his trail. At curbside, Creedmore stumbled and almost fell. There was no way Emil could not feel sorry for the man, murderer though he might be. Think of the guilt on his mind. Get this over with, Emil prayed. Save yourself the suffering. Confess.

Spritzer, the priest, and Jiggsy Potoff all exchanged greetings and handshakes. Emil heard Potoff say something cheerful about having to get back to The Cities and pack for a trip to the Virgin Islands.

Then Potoff and the priest disappeared inside the motel, leaving Eugenio Spritzer there outside the door. The tiny Right-to-Lifer turned back toward his car, then his sharp eyes spotted Emil. Spritzer walked vigorously over to the Chev. He looked dapper, even elegant, in a very pricey camel's hair overcoat.

"How you doing, Eugenio?" asked Emil, rolling down a window partway.

"You're not supposed to be here," accused Spritzer. "It was part of our agreement with Father Rogers."

"Didn't know you were even in on any agreement," Emil drawled.

"There are things coming to you for what you're doing, Emil."

"Is that a threat?"

"No, that's a promise."

"Why did Father Creedmore try to kill the boys too?" Emil prodded. "That's the one thing I can't figure out. What did he have against the boys?"

"He didn't kill anybody," Spritzer declared, "but even if he had, there would have been a good reason!"

"Are you sure you were an orderly up there at St. Concepta's, not an inmate?" Emil asked him.

Spritzer stalked back to his Lincoln.

Emil watched him go. Strange guy, all right. One of the new generation, pushy, contentious, self-righteous. The type of fellow who figured that history had begun at the moment of his birth, and who started jumping up and down if he didn't get what he wanted *right now!* Guys like that had no respect for the old days, or for the people who had endured and survived those times. Like Emil, Nubs, Sarah. Like Mott and Elvira. Like Bundeswehr, even.

You wouldn't have seen this kind of messy murder situation in the old days either, Emil reflected. Back then, everybody knew what the rules were, and they knew the consequences if those rules were broken. Even an itinerant card sharp up from The Cities was smart enough to figure he'd better not get caught cheating. Those dour old farmers took a nickel *seriously.* And if you were crazy enough to interfere with somebody's land or kin, you could bet your hip boots and old grandma's butter churn that you'd wake up way back in the Big Woods with an extra hole in your head. Nobody would mourn your damnfool carcass, either.

But things had changed. Hardly anyone remembered the basic rules, and so you had a lot of unnecessary conflict and consternation. Modern times, Emil thought. Creedmore and Spritzer. Corky and Loftis and Tulip and Trixie Miggs.

Emil waited some more. Finally Father Creedmore stumbled out of the exit door and, like a buck with a 30.06 slug deep in his flesh, faltered toward the Lincoln. A minute later, the blue car was gone, across the parking lot, turning onto the highway back toward Silverton.

Jiggsy Potoff waved from the second-floor window and

Emil got out of his car, entered the motel, and went on up. The room was standard Holiday Inn: twin beds, flowered bedspreads and curtains, innocuous prints on the walls. Polygraph monitors were strewn across one of the beds and an armband was draped over the back of a chair. Long rolls of graph paper marked with the squiggling peaks and valleys of Peter Creedmore's pulse and heartbeat lay on the dressing table like a wrinkled corpse.

"He flunked it," Potoff said, showing Emil the damning evidence. "Look, here's where I asked him his name, if he was a priest, obvious things like that. The control questions, we call them. You'll note that the lines on the graph are regular and even."

Emil nodded.

Using a pencil, Potoff pointed to a series of wild fluctuations where the lines squiggled and lurched almost off the top and bottom of the paper. "Here's where I asked him if he carried a weapon with him on the murder night, if he had moved the evidence deliberately, if he had ever had sex with Mrs. Miggs . . ."

"And the main question?" prodded Emil.

Potoff frowned. "Yes," he said, pointing. "Here's where I asked him if he killed Trixie Miggs."

The lines on the graph wavered madly.

"He denied it, Emil. But the machine caught him."

"You're sure?"

"As sure as the machine can be. He was lying, Emil."

Emil sat down on a leather-upholstered chair of vague Scandinavian design, and stared out the window. The land, broken by tree lines, stretched flatly into the west, fields of snow glittering under the sun.

"Well, there you have it," said Jiggsy Potoff, gathering up and packing his gear.

"The question is what to do with it. What do you think?"

"I think Father Peter Creedmore just failed a polygraph test. There are a few wrinkles, of course. He lied with aplomb about not having been in a mental clinic. I'd say he can't face the fact in his own mind. He's convinced himself he never was a mental patient, while we know for sure that he was."

"Wouldn't that fact throw off the rest of the responses too?"

There was a soft, tentative knocking at the door.

"Come in," Potoff said sharply.

The door opened and Corky Withers entered, looking just as worried as he had all morning. "How'd it go?"

"I figure the guy who just took this polygraph test ought to be brought in and booked, on suspicion at least," Potoff said.

For once, Corky didn't do his usual routine about outsiders and how they shouldn't come in and tell Stearns County people what to do. "What do you think, Emil?" he asked instead.

"Well, let's consider those responses, Corky. First off, calling a spade a spade, Father Pete is a liar."

"What? What do you mean?"

"Look, unless the guy can't remember he was a mental patient, which would mean he's still sick, he's lying. The machine says so."

"Maybe Father didn't *think* he was a mental case," Corky offered.

"Great," said Jiggsy Potoff. "How many of them do?"

"And this says Father had sex with Trixie?" Corky gurgled, wiping sweat from his forehead.

"Somehow," Potoff said, "he managed to score an indeterminate on a few things, but right here in black-and-white we have strong indications of a sexual relationship with the deceased woman. Sheriff Withers, the priest should be placed under arrest."

"Tell me," asked Emil, "did he fiddle with that rubber band he wears on his wrist?"

"That's another thing," Potoff replied. "Something like

that, which is a form of quirky, compulsive behavior, reveals a troubled personality. Yes, he played with the rubber band. In fact, he broke it just when I was attaching the monitors."

Corky stared at the graphs. He was devastated. "What am I going to do now?" he asked.

Outside, Potoff opened the trunk of his car and put the polygraph equipment inside. He slammed the trunk lid and faced Emil. "Well, Merry Christmas."

"Not *him*," moaned Corky.

Roy Riley's black Dodge van rolled across the lot and stopped next to Corky and the other two men. Riley rolled his window down and leaned out. "What's the news today?" he asked.

"How'd you know we were here?" snapped Corky defensively.

"I was driving by and I saw Emil's car back here. I also saw your two-toned Stearns County One at the front entrance."

"Oh."

"What you need, Sheriff," goaded Riley, "is a camouflage net for your car."

"Don't get too smart, Riley. You're not indispensable."

"Neither are you," the reporter shot back.

"I got to go," Potoff interjected. "Long drive home and tomorrow's Christmas Eve. You boys need any more from me or Leander, just give a jingle."

He got into his car, started it up, waved, and drove off.

"Congratulations on getting your scrambler, Sheriff," said Riley, without enthusiasm.

"How'd you know about that?" demanded Corky.

"I got assigned to cover the meeting of the Board of Commissioners. What're you two doing here at the Holiday Inn?"

"No comment," said Corky.

"Yeah," replied the reporter resignedly. "Emil, I'll be out of town for about a day on an assignment. See you." He lifted his hand and drove away.

Corky was smirking in triumph.

"Haven't seen you looking this happy since you won the catechism contest," Emil wondered.

"Riley's off our backs now, Emil," Corky exuded. "Father Rogers had the idea. He suggested that we threaten Riley with the impoundment of his van. Riley didn't care for that one bit, which leads me to believe he's got some illegal equipment in there. Also, we ran a background check on him. Father Rogers' idea too. Riley was arrested once, in Park Ridge, Illinois, outside Chicago."

"What for?"

"Assault."

Riley was a hefty guy. It was possible. Also an aggressive reporter. Might have gotten into a fight. "Disposition?" Emil asked.

"Went to trial and was found not guilty," said Corky, not too happily. "But it goes to show you."

"All right, Corky. Are you going to arrest Father Creedmore? Or should I?"

"Don't you—shouldn't you check with the Chancery first, and tell them how the test went?"

"Oh, I'm sure they'll find out anyway from *somebody* or other," Emil replied acidly. "You are going to make the arrest, though, aren't you?"

"Oh, I will, I *will*. Something's got to be done by tomorrow morning, anyway. That's when the KSTP-TV crew will be back up here in Stearns."

"Keep me posted," Emil told him. He got into his car, left the motel lot, and drove back home along Division Street. Passing the Dippi-Freeze, he was surprised to see Bishop Bundeswehr's Imperial parked in back. Immediately, he sensed that something was afoot.

There was one place in town sure to provide the pulse-beat of St. Cloud's shadowy, subterranean heart. So, since it was about lunchtime, Emil parked across the street from the courthouse and caned his way into the Bar and Grill, where assorted movers, shakers, and hangers-around quaffed beer, wolfed sandwiches, and exchanged the news and rumors they knew about or had invented.

The boys were having a high old time. Emil could hear them laughing and shouting as he approached the door. But when he entered, when the bar crowd turned to see who'd come in, their high spirits faded quickly to an embarrassed hush, followed by the sporadic babble of people trying to get conversation going again, so Emil wouldn't think something was wrong.

Emil knew something was wrong. He had to call Sarah and tell her that he was lunching downtown, so he dropped a dime in the pay phone, charitably giving the regulars time to recover from his obviously unexpected appearance. The line was busy when he dialed, however, so he hung up.

"Emil!"

"Merry Christmas, Emil."

"Give Emil a beer on me."

The old sheriff took a stool down at the end of the bar, next to the pinball machine, and waved greetings to the courthouse crowd. They were all too friendly, and he noted that none of them held his glance for long.

Alf Laundenbush, the bartender, brought him a mug of Grain Belt draft. "Happy holidays, Emil. On the house."

So things were really bad. In the twenty-two years that Emil had known him, Alf had never dispensed a free beer.

"You feeling sorry for me, or what?" Emil growled.

Alf's sick-cheery grin disappeared. "What are you talking about, Emil? You want a hot roast beef sandwich? We got some real nice hot roast beef."

"I'm getting the feeling that maybe I shouldn't be here."

Alf thought it over, and decided to come clean. "Emil," he said, leaning forward and speaking in a hoarse whisper, "have you gone and got yourself in some kind of trouble?"

Emil sipped some beer. "If I have, I'd be damned glad to know about it."

Alf Laundenbush looked greatly relieved. "God, I'm happy to hear that," he said. "I knew it wasn't true. I know you're too smart of an old codger to destroy evidence. That's what I been telling the regulars here all morning. You better believe it."

Emil didn't believe it.

17

H e knew something was wrong as soon as he saw Sarah's face at the window. If it were getting on toward dark, she'd be watching for him. But it was only early afternoon. Besides, he didn't like the set of her lips, sort of droopy and downturned. That was not Sarah.

Yet it wouldn't do to come straight out and ask what the matter was. She'd never tell him. Sarah was not one to go around bellyaching about her private worries. Emil was pretty much the same way. What the hell good did bellyaching do?

"I tried to call," he said, hanging up his overcoat. "Had a quick sandwich at the Bar and Grill. Line was busy. Phone off the hook?"

"Yes," said Sarah, in a small voice, and went into the kitchen. Emil reconnoitered with a glance around the doorjamb. He saw unwashed breakfast dishes. Major catastrophe here, he figured.

"More of those calls?"

Sarah was running water into the sink.

"More of those *silent* calls?" he tried again in a louder voice.

She turned off the tap. "Not so silent today."

Emil sat down in his rocking chair. He got up again and walked into the kitchen.

Sarah began to cry. She stood at the sink, her back toward him, and cried. She didn't make a sound. He could tell she was crying by the tremors in her shoulders.

Sarah had cried maybe half a dozen times in their al-most five decades together. Emil felt a tightness in his gut. "Better tell me," he said. "If you didn't kill somebody, there's nothing we can't handle."

She had cried when their daughter, Susan, had died while still a little girl.

She had cried when the Hannorhed Bank had fore-closed on the farm.

She had cried when her mother died, and when her father passed away.

She had cried when Emil got pneumonia during the winter of '47, and was so badly off that old Father Runde was called to give Last Rites. (Emil was too sick to cry himself that time.)

And she was crying now.

"You didn't kill anybody, did you?" he asked.

Sarah turned to him then, and came to him, and he put his big arms around her.

"Hey, hey," he said gently, as she burrowed soundlessly into his chest. Strange, strange how small she seemed. It must be bad. He steeled himself. Hugh and Dory started off early from Iowa, and had a car crash? Something had happened to Sarah's sister or her husband and kids in Brainerd?

"This is so silly, I'm sorry," she said against his brown suit.

"No, it's not. Tell me."

"It really is silly to cry about this. I guess I wanted it more than I ought to have. Just an honest mistake, that's all it was."

"Well, if that's all it was, what was it?"

Sarah stood back from him a little, and wiped her eyes with his pocket handkerchief. Things were even worse than he had figured. Other than an occasional washing, starching and ironing, that handkerchief had been stick-ing out of his suitcoat pockets for ten years.

"Sister Terence Cooney of the Rosary Society phoned." Sarah faltered. "She said a terrible mistake had been made. The votes actually tallied two hundred and fifteen for Florence Hockapuk and only one hundred and eighty-six for me. I'm not going to be president after all."

So *this* was it! If Emil "harmed" helpless Father Creedmore, Sarah would be wounded in return, powerless to defend herself.

"Bullshit," Emil said.

"I know I'm a fool to get so upset."

"That's not what I mean," said Emil, analyzing the situation.

Sister Terence wouldn't lie about the election like this, not one day before the investiture, not after the story on Sarah had already appeared in the *Trib*, unless she had been told to do so, and there was only one person in town who would tell her to do it.

"Imperial Bill" Bundeswehr.

"It has nothing to do with you," he told Sarah. Bundeswehr had heard about the results of the polygraph test. He was threatened, and he was attacking. Bartender Alf's puzzling remark about "destroying evidence" was a part of it, but Emil could not imagine how. He wondered what else the bishop was planning. There must be plenty more. Emil had been around long enough to know that Bundeswehr had it in him to go off the deep end when he felt himself challenged in the extreme. Bundeswehr had tried and tried to convince farmer Otis Bederbaum of Foley that having two schools, one for the girls and one for the boys, would cut down on sexual contact and thus make better Christians of the children. But frugal Bederbaum had kept exhorting his neighbors, and they'd withheld the money necessary to build the second school. Bundeswehr, furious, had instituted formal excommunication proceedings, which only a cooler head in the Vatican forestalled. Maybe nobody outside Stearns County would believe this had occurred in the twentieth century, but it was true, all right.

Emil had gotten really mad twice in his life. The first time had been in the old days, when he'd been working his rear end off to get up the money to keep Hugh in law school. He'd borrowed Dolph Cragun's cattle truck and taken a dozen hogs to market at the old Stockyards in South St. Paul. Prices had gone up three cents a pound that day, and Emil drove back to Stearns County feeling blessed and rich. He'd stopped off at the Dew Drop in South Haven, to have a little snort and celebrate.

"Well, it's Whippletree, shee-it," sneered big Marv Bauch, as Emil came into the bar.

Emil was in a good mood. "Give old Marv a drink on me," he told Val, the bartender then.

Marv was not in a good mood. "Sure you don't need to keep the dime for your candy-ass brother?" he goaded. "He might need it for school."

"Don't give Marv a drink," Emil told Val.

"Whatsa matter, you won't drink with me?"

Emil was a young guy then, little over thirty, damn strong. "No," he said.

Bauch came over. He was just as strong as Emil.

Val set the beer on the bar. Marv slapped it away. Beer sloshed all over the bar, over Emil. The glass fell on the floor and broke.

"Hey, you guys!" Val said.

Marv sneered. "Don't Hugh know that a Stearns County river-bottom dirt farmer got no business going to school? Does he think he's better than the rest of us? You're throwing your money away, Emil. Hugh is goin' to come back here like all the others, with his ass whipped and his tail between his legs."

Emil couldn't remember much about the fight. All he knew was that he threw a punch, and then another, and finally Val was dragging him away, with Marv Bauch bleeding all over the stained plank floor.

The second time he'd gotten mad was twenty years later, when he'd been a deputy sheriff. St. Cloud had no Negroes—to use the word favored by polite people at the time—but the civil rights movement was just getting under way, and a forward-looking organization in The Cities thought it would be nice to give some of the boondock towns a greater familiarity with interracial harmony. St. Cloud, because of its strong Christian tradition, was chosen as a "target city," and a Negro family was moved into a preselected house on the west side. Naturally, it was the west side, since the north, east, and even the south sides were occupied by the better sort who already knew that "nigger" was not a word to be used in public. The father of this pioneer family was set up in a job with a local industrial concern, the children enrolled in school, and the wife treated to a round of coffee parties with the three women charitable enough to invite her, each of them once on three successive mornings. They made a close foursome, discussing quilt-making, novenas, casseroles, and the weather, all of which were presumed to be highly useful to the newcomer. One of the women was designated to shepherd the "Negro lady" from store to store, so that shopkeepers would not throw her out. All went well until Friday night, when a gang assembled at a west side workingman's bar, discussed the situation in contemplative tones, and proceeded to advance on the preselected house with rocks and baseball bats.

Emil was in the sheriff's office when a call came from the frantic Negro father.

"Let's go," roared Emil, slamming down the phone. "A bunch of thugs are—"

A couple of deputies and old Sheriff Petweiler were sitting around playing poker that night.

"Now, hold on, Emil," Petweiler had said, drawing his

hand close to his chest so the deputies couldn't get a peek. "There ain't no rush. Give it ten minutes or so."

"But there's a gang with baseball bats."

"Emil, it's all *planned*. Nobody's gonna get hurt. This is just to put the fear of the Lord in 'em, know what I mean?"

Emil had driven out there by himself, and stopped the carnage before the house was invaded, although every window was already broken by the time he arrived.

Petweiler and the others came screaming up shortly afterwards—to cover their asses since Emil was already on the scene—and ultimate mayhem was averted.

The Negro family moved out that night.

Emil never carried the west side during all his later campaigns for sheriff.

And now, for a third time, he was mad. At Bundeswehr. At Sister Terence. At Creedmore and Spritzer. At all the rest of them, for having brought about this absurd situation. For having done this hurt to Sarah!

Sarah finished drying her eyes, looking ruefully at the tear-stained handkerchief, now in need of washing, starching, and ironing.

"I'm sorry," she said again.

"What the hell for?" he snarled.

He walked quickly to the phone, scarcely aware of a small lingering twinge in his knee.

"Stearns County Sheriff's Office," whined Alyce. "Good afternoon."

"Alyce, it's me."

"Oh, Sheriff Whippletree! How are you?"

"Not too good. Corky in?"

"Uh-uh. You wanna talk to Jamie Gosch? He's in charge this afternoon."

"Where's Corky?"

"Let's see; ah, he's over at the Chancery right now. You want he should call you back when he comes in?"

"Has Father Creedmore been arrested yet?"

There was a long pause. "What?" asked Alyce. "Why should he be arrested?"

"Forget it, Alyce. Just have Corky call me, okay?"

"Sure thing, Sheriff—I mean Emil. Merry Christmas."

"Damn," he swore, hanging up.

"What now?" asked Sarah, worriedly. She was doing the dishes.

"I'm not sure."

Emil dialed the Chancery. I'm a special deputy, Emil was thinking. I could arrest Creedmore myself.

"Stearns County Diocesan Chancery. Sister Terence Cooney speaking. May I help you?"

"You sure as hell can. This is Emil Whippletree."

"Yes, Mr. Whippletree?"

"I understand you don't count so well," he said.

"Yes, that's right. I'm very sorry. I was never very good in math, you see."

"I want to talk to His Excellency."

"Mr. Whippletree, I'm afraid that won't be possible."

"Why not?"

There was a cold silence on the line for a moment. "He's at an important meeting."

"With Corky Withers?"

"I'm afraid I wouldn't know."

"I don't see why you wouldn't. It doesn't involve mathematics. Give me Father Rogers then."

"He's in the—"

"Don't tell me he's in the meeting."

After some shuffling and hissing on the other end of the wire, Father Rogers answered.

"Hello?"

"It's Emil Whippletree."

"Yes, Mr. Whippletree?" Neutral tone.

"I want to see His Excellency."

"I'm afraid that won't be possible. It *is* the Christmas

season, you know. The preparations for midnight Mass are—"

"Skip it. Maybe you could answer a few questions for me?"

Pause. "I'll certainly try."

"Are you aware that Father Creedmore failed the lie detector test this morning?"

"How could I not be aware of it, Mr. Whippletree, when you have been spreading the word all over? At any rate, it makes no difference. Polygraphs are not admissible as evidence, and His Excellency is going to remain loyal to Father Creedmore."

"Wait a minute," interrupted Emil. "You say *I* have been spreading the word that Father Creedmore flunked?"

"You aren't going to deny it, are you? It's all over the county. You are *persecuting* Father Creedmore, sir. Moreover, you have broken your formal agreement with the bishop to keep this whole matter private. We in Stearns County do not air our dirty linen in public, much less *invent* dirty linen in the first place, as you have done in the case of Father Creedmore."

"I've had about enough of this," Emil declared. "First, I want an appointment with His Excellency right away. Second, I intend to go down to the *Trib* office and put out a few facts for the local citizenry."

"Oh, I don't think you'll want to do that," disagreed Father Rogers.

Something in his voice made Emil cautious. "Why not?"

"Well, His Excellency is a charitable man, and, first and foremost, he has the interests of the community at heart. He wouldn't want to hurt you, either. But is it not true that you received a letter relating to the Miggs homicides? And is it not true that you kept that letter to yourself, not turning it over to the sheriff? And is it not true that you caused the letter to be destroyed?"

"You should be happy. That letter as much as said Creedmore was capable of murder."

Emil remembered the bishop's black Imperial parked outside the Dippi-Freez. Father Rogers had had a heart-to-heart with poor old Dink Kufelski. Emil also remembered Dink in terror of being called to testify about anything. *Emil, I have to live in Stearns County.*

These bastards are really something! Emil realized.

"I seriously doubt if you'd want to make the matter of that letter public," Father Rogers was saying.

They got me by the short ones, Emil thought. "I want an appointment with His Excellency," he demanded again.

Father Rogers considered it. "Perhaps," he decided, with heavy judiciousness. "I'll be in touch."

The line went dead.

Sarah was watching, an anxious look on her face. "What is it? You're not trying to get involved in the Rosary Society election? Emil, don't. Let it rest. It doesn't matter."

Her happy new dress, purchased for the investiture, was draped over the ironing board in the corner of the kitchen.

"It *does* matter."

"Well, yes, but we just have to live with it."

We just have to live with it. That was the old way. Crops failed. *Live with it.* Loved ones died. *Live with it.* Prices went up. *Live with it.* Old age came. Same response. But those things were natural forces. This was different. *Human beings* had taken Sarah's election from her, and *human beings*—so-called—had maneuvered Emil into an humiliating box.

He was still mad. Yet he was torn. It was against his nature to make a big public fuss about anything. Something like that "just wasn't done." Besides, he was in no position to do much of anything now. He *had* kept the letter to himself. He *had* given it back to Dink Kufelski, who destroyed it.

I've got to see the bishop, Emil thought.

He won't see me, Emil knew.

I could be in a mess of trouble, he realized.

He watched TV after supper and tried not to appear restless. Sarah was feeling bad enough about the Rosary Society theft—Emil thought of it as grand larceny—and he didn't want to add to her distress by making his own too evident. But when she went upstairs to take her bath, he crept out to the kitchen phone and called his brother, Hugh.

"Emil? What the hell? I'll see you tomorrow. Something wrong?"

"I think I'm in a pickle."

So Emil told his little brother what had been happening, up to and including Dink Kufelski's letter.

"For Christ sake, Emil, how could you be so *dumb?*" said Hugh, resignedly. "How long were you sheriff?"

"Four terms."

"And didn't even learn what to do with evidence like that? Emil!"

"Am I in bad shape?"

"They've neutralized you, seems to me. Unless you want to make a big thing out of it. Do you?"

"I—I don't know," Emil admitted.

"You really think the priest is the killer?" Hugh inquired.

"I'd still swear to it, from what I've been able to put together."

Hugh didn't answer right away. "Emil," he said then, "me and Dory'll be up there in St. Cloud tomorrow, probably a little after noon, or early afternoon. Weather looks good and roads are clear. Let's talk about it then. I can give you plenty of protection on that letter thing, so don't worry about it. But," he added, after another pause, "it doesn't seem like you to fold up like this."

"I'm not folding up!" What right did little brothers have to say that kind of thing?

"Good to hear it. No sweat. You'll see. You didn't put me through law school for nothing."

"I knew that a long time ago," said Emil.

18

I'm not folding up, thought Emil, trying to get to sleep. Damn, it bugged him. Here he had always taken care of Hugh, and now Hugh would probably have to come up here and take care of him. I'm the big brother, he thought.

He was lying in bed, no longer pretending to be asleep because Sarah, beside him, was finally sleeping. Window blinds were drawn but, even so, moonlight and snowshine seeped into the bedroom, wavering, eerie, half-magic. It was pretty, but strange. Emil lay in bed, thinking about the past.

Fold up, and let it be? Or fight? If fight, for what? What was there to be gained, this late in life, by fighting?

He was shocking grain out on the old home place, down there in the humid Mississippi Valley, south of Clearwater. Itching from chaff and dust, sweating, panting in the heat, he limped to the shade of a chokecherry tree. He saw Hugh slowly walking toward him over the gold-stubbled, heat-shimmering earth of home. Hugh had just graduated from high school.

Hugh was carrying a tin bucket. The pail was so cold that it gave off vapor in the still hot air of the Valley. "Hey, Emil, got some cold lemonade here. You want some?" Emil drank a quart before stopping. Hugh sat down next to him in the dry grass beneath the tree. "Emil, I want to get out of here. I don't want to farm and I don't want to drive a truck and I don't want to waste my life working at a store or factory in St. Cloud. I want to be a lawyer," Hugh said. "It'll take a long time. I'll work. But these are hard times, and I might need somebody to fall back on." Emil sat there for a long time under the choke-cherry tree, sipping the lemonade slowly now. "Go ahead," he told his little brother. "I'll help you all I can." Hugh hadn't said thanks. "You're a good man, Emil," he'd said instead. That was his thanks.

Well, Hugh'd become the lawyer he wanted to be, Emil had lost the farm he wanted to keep, turned into a small-town lawman almost by chance. He and Hugh were in the same line, sort of. Emil seemed to have screwed up this time, though.

He was thinking that maybe he ought to back off the Creedmore thing, take whatever gratuitous lumps they would give him, keep Hugh out of it, let it go, when he heard, outside, from far away, a noise he'd heard before.

There it was again; the loose crosslink of the chain banging inside a fender. Eugenio Spritzer was passing through the neighborhood.

Eugenio Spritzer was not just passing through. Emil could hear the low, powerful growl of the Lincoln's engine, idling on the street outside his house. Slowly, not wanting to wake Sarah, he sat up.

Outside, a car door opened. Emil waited. The car door did not slam shut. Emil shivered, not knowing why. He heard the crunch of footsteps in the crusty snow.

Barefooted and in his pajamas, Emil slipped out of bed and walked to the window. He lifted the shade a couple of inches and peered out. The night was illuminated by snowshine, and it was not difficult to see Spritzer, dwarfish in his thick camel's hair coat, fumbling to insert a key into the trunk lock at the rear of the Lincoln.

The driver's door of the big blue car was open, and the interior lights were on. There was no passenger.

Then Spritzer got the trunk open. Emil watched. Spritzer reached into the trunk compartment and took from it what appeared to be a bottle of wine or liquor, the cap or cork of which he screwed or jerked off and tossed back into the trunk. Then, glancing around, he reached into his coatpocket, pulled out a white handkerchief, and stuffed a portion of it into the neck of the bottle. Eugenio Spritzer held in his hand a Molotov cocktail, a firebomb, and he was staring at Emil's house, almost as if he could see the old sheriff crouched there behind the window sill.

No time for Emil to put on his robe. Already Spritzer was advancing toward the Whippletree house. Emil's service .45, disassembled and wrapped in oilcloth, was in the attic. His hunting weapons, their firing pins removed, were inside locked racks in the basement. The only weapon he had was his cane, which he seized on the run, racing down the stairs to the front door, unmindful of his fragile knee. He threw open the door and stepped out onto the porch. He didn't even feel the below-zero cold.

Spritzer stood twenty feet from the porch, in the snow on Emil's front yard. He held a bottle with its handkerchief-wick in one hand and a silver cigarette lighter in the other.

"Hello, Emil." The cigarette lighter flared.

Emil raised his cane.

"Sorry, Emil. You butted in where you weren't wanted. We won't let you destroy Father."

"He's a sick man. He needs help."

Slowly, Spritzer moved the flame toward the bottle.

"I can throw this cane faster than you can throw that bomb," Emil said.

Spritzer halted, looked at the sheriff.

"Right," said Emil. "Let's say I throw it right now. If I hit you, you might lose your balance. Could turn you into Joan of Arc right here on my front lawn."

Spritzer snapped the cover of the lighter shut, and the fire was extinguished.

"Drop the bottle," Emil said.

Spritzer hesitated. Emil started down the steps, his cane still raised. He did not feel the cold through his flannel pajamas, nor the snow beneath his feet. He felt as if he were soaring and free.

Spritzer backed away a step or two and fell down. He managed to keep the bottle upright.

"Give me the lighter, Eugenio," demanded Emil, standing over him.

Spritzer's eyes were wide and terrified.

"Emil, no," he quavered.

"You were ready to firebomb my house. Now, hand over that lighter or I'll break your face. Don't think I won't."

Emil made the cane whistle a time or two.

"Emil, we're both Christians," Spritzer blithered.

"Is that right? The lighter, Eugenio."

The little man handed it up.

"Now set the bottle down next to you in the snow."

Spritzer did so.

"Stand up. Take off your coat."

Spritzer obeyed.

"Drop your coat on the snow next to the bottle. Take out your billfold and drop it next to your coat."

Emil had the cane raised, and he was ready to slam it as hard as he could if this cowardly bastard made a wrong move. Spritzer did as he was told.

"Nice coat," said Emil, stepping onto it. He was beginning to feel the cold now, and knew he had to get inside pretty soon. "Now I have your coat," he said, "and your ID, and a bottle of gasoline with your fingerprints all over it. You can go now."

Spritzer hesitated.

"I said, get out of here. You make me sick."

Like a terrier in panic, Spritzer hustled to the car. He opened the door, leaped inside, and the Lincoln spun momentarily on the snow, then roared away, the open lid of the trunk still flapping. Emil hurled his cane after the vehicle, picked up the coat, bottle, billfold, and went inside.

"Having trouble sleeping?" asked Sarah drowsily when Emil slid back into bed.

"Not any more," he said.

19

Emil slept peacefully, slept a little later than usual on the morning of Christmas Eve day, although he had many plans. He woke, then lay in bed a while listening to Sarah puttering around downstairs. He heard the *thwack* of the *Trib* against the front door, heard Sarah open and close the door. Then she was hurrying up the stairs.

"Oh, Emil!" she cried, coming into the bedroom and raising the shades so fast that they snapped and spun on the rollers.

"Don't worry," he grunted, sitting up. "Whatever it is, it's nothing. I got everything under control now."

Well, maybe.

WHIPPLETREE INVADES
THE MIGGS MURDER CASE

Mrs. Trixie Miggs and her son were buried yesterday. The Reverend Rogers officiated at the joint funeral. The investigation into their deaths continues. According to reliable Stearns sources, Emil Whippletree, four-term occupant of the sheriff's office mishandled and caused to be destroyed a letter that might have served as evidence of the murderer's identity. . . .

Sarah was watching him. "I thought you'd be more upset."

"Hell no." Emil got out of bed. "I got it under control. Believe me. Say, how about a couple of eggs for breakfast?"

Sarah was puzzled by his feisty mood, in the face of what she had considered another disaster. "You already had your eggs this week. Doc said—"

"I don't give a damn what Doc said. Sorry. Just, how about the eggs? And don't worry. Everything is going to be fine."

Sarah gave him a puzzled look, but went downstairs. Emil got dressed, feeling good. He had the coat, the billfold, and the Molotov cocktail in the garage. Spritzer and Creedmore were probably shitting bricks.

Sheriff Corky Withers phoned while Emil was mopping up the last of his egg yolk with a piece of toast.

"Emil, the KSTP-TV crew will be here in a couple of hours."

"Have fun," the old sheriff grunted. "You did real good last time. Fact, you're pretty good at talking to the local newspaper too."

"Emil, wait. I have something to say. I mean, to you and TV. I'm going to resign."

It took Emil a couple of seconds to register this startling piece of information. "Come again on that?" he asked.

"I'm quitting. Really. That story about you in this morning's *Trib* is only part of it."

"You weren't the 'reliable source' or the 'unnamed county official'?"

"No."

Emil believed him.

"You don't have to resign," Emil said.

"They're not playing *fair!*" Corky complained. His voice was shaky. He was under a lot of strain. "What they've done to you is only part of it. All my life, really, all my life I've believed that they know best, that when the word comes down, a smart person follows along. That way, everything works out. But now it's not—but this is not—*fair!*" he concluded.

"Why don't you go out and arrest Father Creedmore, if you turned such a corner in your life?"

Corky didn't say anything.

"Well, what is quitting, even on KSTP, going to do? I wouldn't quit, if I were you. I'm not quitting. Matter of fact, soon's I finish my coffee, I'm going to drive on over and have a little chat with His Excellency. What time is that TV crew scheduled to show up?"

"Ten-thirty. Maybe eleven. Why?"

"At your office?"

"Yes."

"Maybe I'll be down there to say a few things myself."

"But what should *I* say?"

"You have to decide that for yourself. Why don't you tell them you're going to arrest Peter Creedmore?"

"Well, I—"

"Corky," said Emil, "you're on your own now. Just let me say one more thing. If I bring you absolutely incontrovertible evidence, which means a flat-out admission of guilt, will you arrest the murderer then?"

Corky sighed. "You'll never get that, Emil. Why should Creedmore confess? The biggest gun in town is backing him. The rest of us are pikers."

"If I get an admission, Corky?"

A pause. "Okay." Corky didn't seem to think he was risking much. "So I won't resign. At least not right now."

"I appreciate the gesture though," said Emil. "Good luck on TV."

Emil figured the bishop wouldn't go into his Chancery office on Christmas Eve, so he drove straight over to the mansion near the river. Another clear, cold day, extraordinarily still.

He parked his old Chevrolet on the side of the circular drive, got out and walked to the door. His knee felt fine now, but he made a mental note to hunt for the cane on the street outside his house where he'd thrown it last night. The damn thing about arthritis was that, like an insurance salesman, it kept coming back.

He thumped the big gold knocker a couple of times. Father Creedmore's mother, smiling dazedly into bright sunlight, opened the door. "You'll have to go around in back," she said.

Was Creedmore staying here? Emil stepped into the house and swung the door shut behind him. "Tell His Excellency Sheriff Whippletree is here to see him."

"Yes," she agreed. "Who?"

"The sheriff."

"Oh. Yes." Mrs. Creedmore looked at him doubtfully, and scurried away.

She reappeared in a moment, trailed by a housekeeper wearing an apron liberally stained by silver polish and a towel wrapped around the curlers in her hair. The towel had slipped and the hollow ends of the curlers looked, to Emil, like the muzzles of ranked rocket launchers. As the housekeeper advanced toward Emil, she lost the fuzzy, formless look and assumed the shape of Florence Hockapuk, proud president-elect of the Rosary Society.

"Why, Emil!" she cried, "I guess you're wondering what I'm doing here."

He said yes, he sure was curious.

"Some of us women in the Rosary Society are here helping prepare for the reception after midnight Mass. I'm," she gestured proudly at the stains on her apron, "doing the silver. You and Sarah *will* be attending, won't you?"

"Wouldn't miss it. Do you know if the bishop is in?"

"He wants to see His Excellency," Mrs. Creedmore explained to Mrs. Hockapuk.

Florence Hockapuk veiled her expression quickly, but for just an instant she looked alarmed. "Why, I don't know—" She faltered.

"He's here, isn't he?" Emil demanded.

"I don't—no, he's not," said Florence.

"Oh, yes, he is!" chirped Peter Creedmore's daffy, harmless mother.

Then Father Rogers strode heavily into the room, his bald pate gleaming, his frizzy, receding hair a red halo.

"What's going on here—oh"— this with distaste —"Mr. Whippletree. Ladies, thank you," he added.

The two women retreated, Florence Hockapuk with obvious reluctance.

"Well?" sniffed Father Rogers.

"I'm here for my appointment," said Emil.

"You don't *have* an appointment."

"I do now. Get Imperial Bill down here."

"Sir, I know you're disappointed about your wife losing the—"

"Father," said Emil, "I wouldn't want to talk to anybody like I'm about ready to talk to you. You go tell His Excellency I've got Eugenio Spritzer's fingerprints on a firebomb. I've been wondering if they'll match the unknown prints on two guns found in the Miggs' closet. Am I making myself clear enough for you?"

Emil had never seen anybody as startled as Father Rogers was then.

Within minutes, Wilhelm Bundeswehr descended the staircase from the second floor. His tread was heavy. He wore a cardinal-red dressing gown and chewed a dead cigar.

"Emil," he gurgled, offering neither his hand nor his ring. "You want to talk?"

"That's the general idea."

The bishop led Emil through the big room with the red draperies—no jokes about them today—and into a small, tidy office. Motioning Emil to a chair, the bishop took a seat behind his desk, lit the stub of cigar, ducked his head, scowling, toward Emil. Fat folds of flesh around his jaw rippled, one into another.

"All right, Emil. Speak your piece."

Emil nodded. "First off, Sarah will be invested president of the Rosary Society tonight."

Bundeswehr looked up, surprised. "What are you talking about, Emil?" The old cleric looked genuinely perplexed, but then he had always been one hell of an actor.

"Don't tell me you don't know?" Emil said. "Sister Terence called Sarah and told her there'd been a mistake on the vote. Said Florence Hockapuk had won. How could something like that happen without your knowing about it?"

A clump of nerves below Bundeswehr's left eye was quivering. "Remember what I told you about subordinates?" he growled, pressing a button on his phone console. "Some of them get a little overzealous."

In moments, Father Rogers appeared at the door. "Yes, Your Excellency?" His face was blank and smooth. His voice was the purr of a cat.

"Emil tells me some sort of mix-up has occurred with regard to this Rosary Society vote. You know anything about that?"

"I'm sure I don't," said Father Rogers, his eyes as wide and innocent as a Panda's.

"Soon as that first story appeared in the *Trib*," Emil interjected, looking at the priest, "I got a call that threatened Sarah in sort of a roundabout way. Threatened *Sarah* because somebody thought *I* was gonna get too deeply mixed up in the case. Well, I met Spritzer a little later on—out at Father Creedmore's, to be exact—and I recognized his voice as the one I'd heard on the phone. Does Spritzer know Sister Terence pretty well, or what?"

"I'm sure I could find out," offered Father Rogers, looking as clever as a monkey.

"Are you sure you don't know anything about this?" His Excellency asked the priest.

"No, not at all," said Father Rogers, slick as the shit of a day-old calf.

"'That'll be all, Father," said the bishop, waiting until his chancellor withdrew to say, "Sister Terence made a horrible mistake, but it's too late."

"No. Sister Terence made no mistake, and we both know it. Sarah gets invested. Before midnight Mass. At St. Mary's Cathedral. By you. Tonight."

Bundeswehr chewed his cigar, blew a puff of smoke or two. His little eyes glittered with the effort of calculation.

"In return for what?" he asked.

"In return for nothing."

The bishop didn't say yes, but he didn't say no. Father Rogers had already told him about Spritzer's fingerprints. He was off-balance.

"It won't be hard," Emily said. "The story on Sarah's election has already been in the *Trib*. This business about a miscount and everything isn't generally known. You'll be able to do the right thing easily."

Bundeswehr tilted his head to one side and removed the cigar. The end of it glistened darkly, like a thick black teat. "What else?"

"Father Creedmore should be arrested."

The bishop shook his head. "Can't permit that, Emil. How would it look?"

"How would it *look*? How do you think it looks now?"

"Only to you. And maybe a few others. Emil, I've got to think of the community here. The *community*, Emil. Why, if the news got out—no, it would be too shattering. The people couldn't handle news like that, like the arrest of a priest. No."

"The people can handle a lot more than you give them credit for."

"No, they can't, Emil. They haven't been trained for certain truths."

"Whose fault is that?"

"It's nobody's fault. A people kept innocent stands a better chance of salvation."

"They're also more easily led."

"You'll ruin the county, Emil. Things have been so good for so long. The old ways, Emil. Hard work. Decency. Fear of the Lord. Prayer."

"That's Stearns County?"

"Yes."

"Seems to me you're willing to use some pretty bad tactics to preserve all those good things."

Bundeswehr chewed at his cigar and looked away.

"Let's take a look at specific evidence," Emil told him. "When Father Creedmore took the polygraph test, it revealed he'd had a weapon with him in his car."

Bundeswehr raised his hand. "I've already covered that matter with Father Pete. He meant that he had the weapon of his *faith* with him, that's all."

"But he *denied* having a weapon."

"Some people wouldn't understand the concept of faith as a weapon, Emil. Father's thought processes are very complex. And when he seemed to admit having had sexual relations with Mrs. Miggs, he was only denying a secret desire. We're none of us immune to the weaknesses of our natures, Emil. Father Pete was in a panic when he took that test, and the lust in his heart, which tormented him frightfully, caused him to answer as he did."

"So he felt just as guilty about desiring Trixie Miggs as he would have if he'd actually gone ahead and done it with her? I suppose he denied killing her because he might once have wished her dead?"

"You put it aptly. Your machine can't measure the subtleties involved. He feels *very* strongly about abortion."

"So how come Father Creedmore tainted the evidence in the Miggs house when he gave last rites?" Emil demanded. "There was no need for him to do that."

The bishop smiled sadly. "That's a complicated question, Emil."

"I'll try and figure out any answer you may give me, Bishop."

Bundeswehr examined his manicured fingernails and his big ring of office. "Emil, what I'm about to tell you can't leave this room."

"We've done that before. No deal." Emil stood up.

"Where are you going?" Bundeswehr asked, with veiled alarm.

"Over to Corky's office. KSTP-TV will show up soon. I've got some things to say. Not everybody's going to believe me, but I did solve the Koster case some years back, and plenty of people will listen to me."

"About what?" Bundeswehr seemed to realize that Emil would actually make good his threat, tradition against the airing of dirty linen notwithstanding. "You've no incontrovertible proof that Father Pete is a killer."

"Well, I damn sure know Father Pete oughtn't to be in a position of responsibility. I'll draw some pictures for TV, and let people make up their minds."

The bishop bit his cigar stub almost in two, discarded it in an ashtray on his desk. "Sit down, Emil," he said.

The old sheriff did, slowly, as if he might get up again at any second.

"Emil, I talked everything over with Father Pete. And I mean *everything*. I'm his confessor, you know."

"So you can't say anything about it."

Bundeswehr looked irritated, then pained. "No, Emil, he and I discussed things man-to-man. He told me that he fouled the evidence in the house because he was afraid that Eugenio was the killer. Eugenio is the only real friend Father Pete has. I didn't fully realize it until I made some inquiries. I said I'd check, remember? And I did. Chancellor Rogers knew I was concerned about Father Creedmore. He also knows that I'm a staunch Right-to-Lifer. What he *didn't* know is that I have long regarded Eugenio Spritzer with—how can I phrase this charitably? Well, I think he's a jackass, frankly."

"And now you know."

"And now I know."

Emil gave the matter some quick calculation. Spritzer might easily have taken Father Creedmore's Chrysler Le-Baron on the night of the murders, driven to the Miggs house, and committed the crime. Nubs Tufo had been close enough to the car to get the license plate number. Might he also have seen—could he also remember—whether the figure behind the steering wheel was large, like Creedmore, or small, like Sprtizer? Was there some way Nubs could be made to remember? Hypnotism? Some drug?

"If Spritzer is Father Creedmore's only friend," Emil said, "then he's going to be mighty lonely, isn't he? I could put Eugenio away on a five-to-ten year conviction for the firebomb thing."

"I'll get rid of Spritzer, Emil. Don't you worry about that. Right-to-Lifers, by and large, are good people. But any group that believes strongly in a cause always has a radical fringe of five or ten percent. It's guys like Sprtizer who pander to this element, and make the movement look bad. Spritzer'll be out of town by tomorrow, Emil."

"But he shouldn't have been holding the job he has!"

"Let me be the judge of that, Emil. He won't be, not after tonight."

"What is Mrs. Creedmore doing here, by the way?" Emil asked.

"Father Pete is very upset. He didn't want her to see him in his present state."

"I can believe it." Emil was wondering whether to tell Bundeswehr of his plan to tie Spritzer to the Miggs house on the night of the murders. He decided against it. Bundeswehr had an administrator's natural facility for using every morsel of information to his own advantage.

"I want you to leave Father Creedmore alone, Emil. No more investigation. No TV announcement. Just let him alone. You'll never know, not with sufficient certainty, that he is the killer."

Emil recognized the bishop's bid. Drop the Creedmore investigation, let the Miggs case lie.

"And Sarah gets the presidency?"

Bundeswehr nodded. "Mistakes do happen."

Emil laughed dryly, without humor. "Mistakes! You just lost your temper, is all. Like the time poor old Otis Bederbaum made you mad and you wanted to excommunicate him. Only this time you picked on my wife, in order to get *my* goat. Well, I want you to know that I think it's pretty damn low."

Bundeswehr flushed darkly. Emil summed up the situation for himself. It was true that he did not have absolute proof on Creedmore. But he wasn't about to quit trying, and he was in no way prevented from going after Eugenio Spritzer. I got to see Nubs Tufo right away, he thought.

"And, naturally, you won't go over to the sheriff's office for the TV show," Bundeswehr added.

"No deal. That firebomb lets me call the shots. You call Sarah and apologize for everything."

His Excellency frowned. He was not disposed by training or temperament to apologize for anything.

"And you see to it that Sister Terence Cooney calls to apologize too. She's the type that gives good sisters a bad name."

Bundeswehr lifted his chins defiantly, losing some rolls of fat.

"You call right now," Emil said, pointing to the phone on the bishop's desk. "You apologize to Sarah, over the phone, in my presence."

Bundeswehr was still thinking it over.

"We don't want any dirty linen aired," Emil said, heavy on the piety. "This is Stearns County, after all."

"What's your phone number, Emil?" asked the bishop wearily, lifting the receiver.

"Ask Eugenio Spritzer." But Emil gave him the number.

"Mrs. Whippletree? Bishop Bundeswehr. I know you must be busy, day like today, but I'm calling to clear up a terrible batch of miscue and confusion."

The old bastard is a real charmer, reflected Emil, as he listened to the bishop give Sarah this gigantic snowjob about how the vote for president of the Rosary Society had gotten so screwed up.

"So I'll look forward to seeing you at St. Mary's tonight, Mrs. Whippletree," Bundeswehr concluded.

An expression of sheer disbelief crossed his fat face then. He covered the receiver with his hand, and stared at Emil in dismay. "Your wife says she's not interested in the position any more."

Good for you, Sarah, Whippletree thought. "Ask her to change her mind for the good of the community," he said.

Bundeswehr frowned, but he did as he was told.

"Ah, thank you, Mrs. Whippletree," the bishop said, after listening a moment, "I knew I could count on you."

Bundeswehr hung up, stood up. So did Emil.

"That's that," the bishop said. "See you at midnight Mass?"

"Sure thing. My brother'll be there too. He and his wife are coming for a visit. He's a lawyer. Pretty sharp one, I think."

Bundeswehr's brows beetled a bit. He couldn't tell if Emil had mentioned Hugh's profession for any particular reason, and he was still on his guard.

He held out his hand to Emil, the ring facing upward.

Emil shook his hand.

20

The new battery in Emil's car started her up like a dream. It was encouraging to find something modern that actually worked. He checked his watch. Couple of minutes after ten. He had a few hours before his brother would show up, and he knew how to spend them.

He thought about a lot of things while driving the familiar route to Silverton. Strange how quiet the land became at Christmastime. The gentle feeling was almost holy, communicating its aura to the old sheriff, who had loved this country nearly as long as anybody, and a lot better than most.

He felt good about his encounter with Bishop Bundeswehr, mainly because he'd gotten Sarah what was due her. Too bad about old Florence Hockapuk. She could stew in her own juice! Emil still *knew* Father Creedmore had been involved in the murders, and Bundeswehr had certainly wasted no time in asserting that he could rid Stearns County of Spritzer by tomorrow. Not if I find out he's the killer, Emil vowed.

Believing that he would get the incontrovertible proof, the admission of guilt he was seeking, Emil drove through Silverton—both Creedmore's Chrysler and Eugenio's Lincoln were parked in the rectory driveway—turned left at the stop sign, and headed toward Tufo's Lake. There were no cars in front of the Goose Step Inn, he observed, but then it was pretty early in the day.

If only Nubs Tufo could just remember a little bit more about what he saw that night.

Roy Riley was on Emil's mind too, however, and he slowed when he spotted Bawlie Wepner's mailbox, turned into the driveway, and stopped. Bawlie's house was locked.

ENTRANCE TO THESE PREMISES IS FORBIDDEN
BY ORDER OF THE STEARNS COUNTY SHERIFF,
Courtney P. Withers, Jr.

Emil thought it over for a couple of seconds, fished around in his overcoat, and withdrew a pocket knife. The lock gave easily after a few twists and jiggles. Bawlie's house smelled sour and stale. The urine-stained blankets were still on the couch. Had Bawlie remained there, he would still be alive. Yet something had troubled his blurred drunk's brain, something about the murders, and whatever it was had been enough to send him out of his house on the night of the storm, to a freezing death in a Minnesota ditch.

Whippletree stood next to the couch, taking in the *feel* of this house, as he had previously permitted the tawdry spirit of the Miggs residence access to his consciousness. There he had sensed implacable rage. Here in Bawlie's place, Emil perceived sadness, hopelessness, the befuddled disbelief of a person who had wanted desperately to be a winner, but who was never able to understand the forces that made him a loser. Oh, yes, Bawlie had been shrewd enough to divine the resentment of his buddies when he'd gone away to be a baseball pitcher. But he'd understood too late the nature of all the "friends" who comforted him, who bought him thousands of consoling drinks when he came back home, a failure.

His failure was their affirmation. Thus the Syndrome was sustained.

Emil walked to the telephone, which was in the kitchen. Had Roy Riley gone out to the kitchen, when

Emil and Nubs were getting Bawlie settled on the couch? Had he done something to the phone, so that Bawlie'd been unable to call Emil? Seemed to Emil that he distinctly remembered Riley in the kitchen, all over the house, looking for blankets.

The point of the knife blade was too sharp for the little screws on the telephone. Emil found a kitchen knife in one of the drawers. It worked fine as a screwdriver, and the plastic housing of the phone came off easily, revealing the mechanism.

Every wire had been neatly snipped.

Riley would know what to do, wouldn't he? Who else would?

Emil pictured old Bawlie, still drunk, trying and trying to dial the phone, finally giving up in disgust and leaving his house. Bawlie, who'd figured out the murderer's identity.

That was why Bawlie hadn't said anything in Riley's presence! He'd tried to, after Riley had gone in search of blankets. But then he'd passed out.

Emil put the housing back on, reinserted and turned the little screws, left the house, and locked it. He was confused. The motives of Creedmore and Spritzer were clear enough. What might have been Riley's motive? The only thing Emil could think of was obvious: Riley was father to Trixie's aborted baby. So? Murder for that?

"Possible," he decided, preparing to get back into his car. Everybody reacts differently to life's big events.

He stood outside his car for a long moment, taking in the scene, enjoying the preternatural stillness of the day. Snow lay deeply on the ground, and sifted down in intermittent powdery cascades from the pine branches where it had settled during the storm. The tragic Miggs house caught Emil's eye, glaring yellow against the whiteness all around.

I'll take one last look, he decided.

Then he was alone in the icy quiet of the murder house. He walked back toward the bedrooms.

The mattresses and sleeping bags were gone. The boys' bedroom was empty. Emil's footfalls echoed hollowly. Pale light, reflected off the lake's ice, shone dully on the walls.

Trixie's room had been stripped, leaving only mattress, bed, chair, and dresser. The plastic statue of the Virgin was gone, and the closet empty of everything, yet the place still reeked of perfume. The scent was heavier, sweeter, than that lemon-lime junk Corky wore. Maybe the two of them should have gotten together after all, Emil thought.

He walked into the kitchen. The room had been thoroughly washed, and everything was neat and clean. The shattered clock held fast at 4:22, something about the time itself nagging Emil, eating away at the back of his brain, like a contagious spore, alien, deadly and acute. He stepped back and stared at the clock again. 4:22. Why did 4:22 keep on gnawing away at his mind? What had happened between 3:30 and 4:22?

Emil thought he heard something, listened, then dismissed it.

A milk truck drove by on the road outside, bound for Clearwater. It would pass the Heiderscheidt place. Wonder how Mott's doing? Emil thought. He heard the sound of another engine, which slowed for a moment, then passed on.

Mott Heiderscheidt. Last rites. Father Creedmore. Not called by Mrs. Heiderscheidt. Went there on his own. 3:30. 4:22, and then . . . 3:30. Time lapse. 4:22, and then . . .

"Hello, Emil."

Whippletree spun around. Roy Riley stood in the kitchen doorway, grim, dog-tired, and tough as nails.

21

"**Y**ou look a sight," Emil said, noting the fatigue on the reporter's hard, round face. "What've you been up to?"

"Away on an assignment. Sort of a self-assignment, you might say. Saw your car here on my way back from the Twin Cities airport. Return to the scene of the crime, huh?"

"I've become real interested in that clock," replied Emil, gesturing toward the ruined wall. "The whole thing about time doesn't check out. Creedmore was at the Heiderscheidt's house at three-thirty. He claimed in his statement to have turned around in the Miggs' driveway on his way to the Heiderscheidt farm. Nubs didn't say definitely, but he recollected seeing the car with Creedmore's license plates here at around four. Creedmore wouldn't have gotten lost on the way *back* from Heiderscheidt's."

Riley stared at the clock. "Are you suggesting there was somebody else?"

"Where's the phone in Bawlie Wepner's house?" Emil asked him.

"What?" asked Riley, looking puzzled. "I don't know. Why?"

"All the wires inside it were cut. Bawlie wasn't *supposed* to make any phone calls. Certainly not to me. Somebody made sure of that."

Riley's eyes widened. "Emil! *Me?* Jesus, you don't think I—"

"Oh, hell no," Emil said. "I'm just trying to give you

some pointers to use when you write the big story on the Miggs case and win back your *Trib* spurs."

"Gee, thanks, Emil," Riley said.

The two men walked outside, and Emil locked the door behind them.

"Say, what was this assignment you were away on?"

"I think you'll be *very* interested," Riley said, as they walked slowly toward the sheriff's car and the reporter's van. "The thing that puzzled me most about Creedmore's career was the Washington, D.C., phase of it. So that's where I went, D.C."

"Hit paydirt?"

"I think so. You know, Bundeswehr is not a bad judge of people, all things considered. So I figured he wouldn't have reassigned Creedmore to a responsible job if he hadn't had some reasonable assurance that the guy was up to the pressure."

"And?"

"Creedmore really did teach Sacred Theology at Catholic U. I checked some outdated course catalogs in the library. I even pretended to be an old student looking for Father Pete, my favorite professor. Couple of faculty members told me he'd gone back to pastoral duties in Minnesota. They seemed to think highly of him, and praised his dedication."

Emil recalled his conversation with Dink Kufelski. What was it that Dink had said? Something about it being hard to know Father Creedmore because you couldn't tell which personality he would show on any given day?

"So you no longer think Creedmore's a suspect?" Emil asked.

"I didn't say that. I don't know."

"What about Eugenio Spritzer?"

Riley snorted. "You're gonna love this, Emil. Spritzer was out there in D.C. *with* Creedmore. All those years. I think he's pretended to be a mascot all along, whereas he's really an *eminence grise*."

"A—what the hell are you talking about?" asked Emil.

"I'm saying that Spritzer's the dominant one in that twosome, and not the other way around. He's quite a guy. I learned that, in D.C., he got to be secretary-treasurer for a Right-to-Life splinter group. The radical fringe, all the way. Rich right-wing radical. He got to handle a lot of dough. He did handle it. Both the Washington dailies carried news of his dismissal."

So that's where Eugenio had gotten his money. "But didn't they prosecute him?"

"Why advertise that contributor's bucks are being skimmed by a professional do-gooder?"

"You know," said Emil, as the reporter climbed into his van and started the engine, "at first I would have bet actual money that Father Pete was my man, now I'm beginning to think it's Spritzer." He debated whether or not to tell Riley about the firebomb, but decided against it for the time being. "You going back to St. Cloud?"

"Yeah," Riley said. "I could use some sleep."

"Okay. See you at midnight Mass. I got to go over and talk to Nubs Tufo. Maybe he can dredge up a little more memory for me to use."

Waving good-bye to the reporter, Emil drove his car down the rutted, twisting road to Nubs Tufo's cabin. He parked in the woods behind it. Nubs' pockmarked pickup truck stood there, covered with a light coating of blown snow. Beneath white birch, a granite stone marked STORMY tilted out of a mound of rocks and frozen sod.

Nubs Tufo came around the corner of his cabin, to see who had driven up.

"I'm finally here for that Tom and Jerry," Emil said, getting out of his car. "You got some time?"

Nubs led Emil into the old cabin. Although crude, with walls of wooden planking and a linoleum-covered

floor, it was scrupulously kept. Steel traps for bear, wolf,
fox, rabbit, muskrat, and mink hung from pegs on the
north wall, not a speck of rust on any of them. At a
workbench near the doorway, skins from the morning's
crop of muskrat dried on wire stretchers. There was a
table with four chairs, all hand-made, and a glowing
Franklin stove on a cement slab in the middle of the
cabin. Nubs' bed, neatly made, stood in a far corner. A
hotplate with double burners, a small fridge, and a sink
took up the south wall.

"Take your coat off, Emil," Nubs grunted. "Glad you
could make it. I'll get the eggs out. Old Mott's gone, I hate
to say."

"Mott?" said Emil. He hung up his coat, took off his
boots. "He wanted to make it through Christmas."

"Yeah. But I seen the hearse go by to fetch him."

Nubs broke half a dozen eggs into a large bowl, then
used a big spoon to lift the yolks to a second bowl, which
he handed Emil, along with an eggbeater. "Here. I ain't
about to do all the work." Putting a kettle of water atop
the Franklin stove, he sat down at the table with Emil,
who was busy beating the yolks into froth. Nubs did likewise with the eggwhites. Neither of them spoke for a long
time. The water in the kettle began to hiss.

"Poor old Mott," Nubs said.

"I saw your dog's stone out there. Sorry. Maybe you
ought to get another dog."

"Might not be around."

"Sure you'll be."

"Never can tell."

Nubs reached over, took Emil's bowl of beaten yolks,
and blended the batter slowly into his frothy bowl of
whipped whites. The water was boiling now. Nubs got up,
fetched two cups and a bottle of brandy. He poured the
cups half-full of brandy, spooned a large dollop of batter
into each, and then poured in hot water. "Nutmeg's right

there next to the pepper and salt shakers," he said, sitting down again.

Emil sprinkled a generous quantity of nutmeg on top of his foaming drink, inhaling the fragrance, and Nubs did likewise. The two men touched cups, drank, and licked batter from their upper lips.

"Can make a Tom and Jerry with rum, too," said Nubs. "But I like brandy better." He looked directly at Emil. "What can I do for you?"

Among the old-timers, it was understood from the outset that no visit was ever totally without some serious purpose. One party or the other, often both parties, had to have a solemn intent, however small, or the meeting would be frivolous, which would constitute a waste of time.

Emil took another long swallow of the hot drink. It was more effective than any antihistamine or sinus spray known to man.

"Night of the murders," he said.

Nubs nodded.

"You saw Creedmore's car?"

Nubs nodded.

"Person inside it. Big or little?"

Nubs thought it over carefully. "Can't remember," he said.

"Long about four A.M., when you were going to check your traps?"

Nod.

"The car headed toward Mott Heiderscheidt's place?"

Another nod.

This is the thing, Emil worried. Creedmore had claimed he'd been at the Miggs house earlier, at 3:30.

Nubs was looking straight at him, waiting for more.

"How'd you get along with the Miggs family?" Emil asked.

Nubs shook his head. "The kids have been robbing my

traps for a couple years now. The woman's boyfriend dumped junk on my property."

"Why didn't you call the law?"

"You and me, Emil, I thought we learned how to take care of ourselves?"

The old sheriff sipped more of his fragrant drink. "How'd Stormy die, Nubs?" he guessed.

"Josh Miggs shot him."

"With a rifle?"

Nod.

"And your pickup?"

"Roger Miggs blasted it with a shotgun."

"What'd you do?"

"I wrestled the guns away from both of 'em, carried the guns up to their house, told their mother what had happened."

"What'd she say?"

"She took the guns back and then told me to go fuck myself."

Nubs Tufo's eyes were hard on Emil's, direct, unwavering and calm.

"Yet," Emil pressed, "when you saw Josh Miggs freezing to death in the woods, you picked him up and carried him out."

Nubs grunted. "Couldn't let Josh freeze to death under a tree when God had already decided he should live. And I can't tell you how bad I feel about Bawlie. Who could've guessed he'd go hunting for a phone after I haywired his? Freshen your Tom and Jerry, hey, Emil?"

Emil said yes. Nubs complied, and poured himself a second as well.

"I been reading eggs is no good for a person," he said slowly, "but they sure do taste nice if you fix 'em right."

"Sure do," Emil agreed, trying to keep his hand steady and his voice from quavering.

"Any more questions, Emil?"

Only one question remained, which Emil could not bear to ask, because he knew what the answer might be. He knew, too, that Nubs Tufo would tell him the truth.

"I sure do want to spend Christmas out here in peace," Nubs drawled. "You could tell Corky I might be driving into St. Cloud to give myself up. About mid-morning. Day after tomorrow. It could happen."

"I'm not telling Corky anything," Emil said.

22

Emil spotted his brother's car parked in the driveway. Good, Hugh and Dory'd had a safe trip up from Iowa. But now Emil wished he hadn't gotten all agitated last night, wished he hadn't phoned Hugh about the Miggs case. He couldn't bear to think about the Miggs case any more.

Two-bit punk brats hounding old Nubs for who knew how long, stealing from his traps, taunting him, marring the final days of his life with their arrogance and stupidity, their mother offending him further. Truck blasted. Dog shot. "Fuck you, Tufo."

Yes, Nubs would have done it, all right. *I* might have done it myself!

He parked his car behind Hugh's and climbed out. Three little kids trudged single-file up the sidewalk. The leader bore Emil's cane like a staff. The crook of the cane was half a head taller than the boy, whose disciples were even smaller than he was. Emil recognized little Timmy Kohler, whose family lived across the street.

"Hello, Timmy. What are you fellows up to?"

"We're the three wise guys. We're goin' to Bethalben."

"After you get there, remember to put my cane on the porch, okay? I might want to make that trip sometime myself."

"Yes, sir."

The boys trudged on.

"Emil!" cried Dory, when he entered the house, and gave him a big hug.

Hugh came over. He and Emil indulged in the rare intimacy of a handshake. Hugh was wearing a neck brace, and he looked embarrassed.

"What the hell is that?" Emil asked.

"Touch of osteoarthritis. Nothing serious. I don't have to wear the brace all the time."

"Age gettin' to you, huh?" Emil grinned.

"Emil!" said Sarah, in her warning voice. She'd tell about his recent knee episode if he wasn't careful.

They took it easy all afternoon, resting up for midnight Mass and a late night out. Sarah and Dory went upstairs to take naps. Emil and Hugh loafed around the living room, sipping a couple of beers, watching TV.

"That murder case you called me about last night," Hugh said finally. "You still in a jam?"

"Looks to be over."

"Sure?"

"Pretty much so." Briefly, Emil told about Father Creedmore, and all the evidence that had pointed to him. He detailed Bishop Bundeswehr's machinations.

"Stearns never changes, does it?" Hugh smiled, shaking his head. " 'Imperial Bill.' "

Then Emil told Hugh about Nubs Tufo.

"Old *Nubs?* I don't believe it. Why, the guy must be— about your age."

"Hey, no need to get personal."

"Aside from what Nubs said, how did you finally fit things together?"

"Put myself in Nubs' place. It's night. He can't sleep. His dog is dead. He's outside in the cold, an old guy with not much time left, undone by strange new people in a changing time. They don't give a damn about him, nor care about what he's gone through, what he knows, what he's carried with him out of the past. Nubs—and a lot of the rest of us—believe we are of *value* because we built this country. That's something these newcomers would never even think of, much less understand.

"Now, Nubs might not have gone ahead with it," Emil continued. "But there he is, outside with his shotgun, when Father Creedmore gets confused on his way to the Heiderscheidt's. Up until that point, Nubs may not have been able to decide whether to do it or not. But Creedmore did come by, and turned around in the drive. Nubs saw that license number, decided he could hide behind it, and went ahead. We know the rest."

"Do you think he could have, Emil?" asked Hugh. "That he really could have gone on living with himself?"

"Who's to say?"

"Think he'll really turn himself in to Corky?"

"Figure he will. Don't know for sure, though."

"What if he doesn't? What will you do?"

"That," replied Emil, "is what I'm trying not to think about."

"Guy like Nubs, he'll expect you to come and get him."

"Guy like Nubs, he will. He knows me and I know him."

After a late supper of salmon loaf, baked potatoes, and cole slaw, the four Whippletrees got ready. Sarah looked splendid in her new dress.

"But I'm nervous as if I had nothing on," she complained, trying to button her coat with trembling fingers. "Oh, my goodness, maybe I shouldn't have run for president in the first place."

"You had to do it for the good of the community," Emil reminded her.

Hugh took off his neck brace. They all went out, got into Emil's car, and drove over to St. Mary's Cathedral. Midnight Mass, celebrated by Bishop Bundeswehr, was one of the biggest events of the Stearns County year, and everybody who was anybody made it a point to crowd into the drafty old church. Due to Sarah's election, however, seats in a pew way up front were reserved, and the Whippletrees did not have to arrive an hour early, like some people did, to get a seat near the altar.

They ran into Corky Withers while climbing the wide steps into the church. He had a new overcoat, and a new hat too, which he tipped toward the ladies. "Emil, can I see you a sec?"

Emil led him behind one of the big stone pillars. "What's up?" He got a powerful whiff of Old Spice. Corky had a new brand.

"Did you get that admission of guilt you were talking about?"

"I'm not sure."

"Any of that incontrovertible proof?"

"What did you say to the TV?"

"I said it would take more time than I'd thought to bring in the killer, but that I'd get him eventually."

"Then you didn't resign?"

"No. You told me not to. You convinced me, Emil, that I'm as good as anybody, and to prove it I'm going to bring in the Miggs killer. I don't care how long it takes. After all, it's my job. That's what you taught me."

"I'm glad," said Emil.

"I want to thank you for your help." Corky stuck out his hand. Emil shook it. "I'm on my own now," Corky said, "so you won't have to hold my hand any more."

Emil released his hand.

"You're a good man, Emil," Corky effused. "You taught me that responsibility is mine!"

Corky seemed in danger of launching into a campaign speech. Emil opted for retreat. He rejoined Hugh and the ladies. They walked slowly up the long center aisle to their pew in front.

Across the center aisle, in the second pew, Florence Hockapuk sat with her husband, Ewald. Florence looked acutely unhappy. She fingered rosary beads, praying away to beat the band. Ewald sat hunched over, with no expression of any kind on his face. Everything seemed as usual with the Hockapuks.

Emil sat there, waiting for the show to begin. Hugh looked around, checking to see how many people he could still identify. Sarah fidgeted and Dory tried to calm her. Finally the organ started up.

Sister Terence Cooney stalked out in a long black habit, cued the Cathedral choirmembers with a thin, flexible wand, and led them in "Silent Night," which was rendered in German in honor of the old pioneers. The nun was as talented in her conducting as she'd been in ballot-juggling.

"Stille Nacht" ended. The last wavering chords of the organ rose to die against a vast, smoky ceiling. The congregation hushed. A bell tinkled. Altar boys, marching in a column of twos, poured through a door near the altar, spread out, and took their positions all about the front of the church. The people stood up. The column of altar boys was followed by a column of priests, resplendent in glorious vestments—the priests spreading out and taking up preassigned positions too—and at last His Excellency, Wilhelm Bundeswehr, appeared. He walked like a king, beamed like Buddha, and bore the staff of his office as if it were a rod to call down lightning from the skies. With his staff, high hat, and bearing, he seemed a medieval wizard clothed in brilliant white, or at least a wise guy on his way to Bethalben.

When Bundeswehr had been escorted to his throne and seated, with a choreography only slightly more complicated than the final act of "Swan Lake," Father Rogers stepped before the congregation.

"It gives me great honor," he said, "to call forward at this time for investiture as new president of our wonderful Rosary Society"—here he paused a long time, smiling with his lips shut—"Mrs."—here he paused again, grinning with his teeth— "Mrs. Sarah Whippletree!"

It would not have been right to applaud in the cathedral, but a wave of good feeling followed Sarah as she went forward, knelt, and kissed Imperial Bill's ring.

Emil kissed her cheek when she returned to the pew, happy tears in her eyes.

Father Rogers was still standing up there by the altar. "Tonight," he announced, "His Excellency is inaugurating a new tradition here in Stearns County, an event that will be annual in nature, the awarding of Father Pierz Layman's Service Medals."

Father Pierz, long dead, had been a pioneer priest who claimed once to have seen a gigantic cross in the sky west of Big Falls, a sighting interpreted immediately and forever after as miraculous.

Father Rogers held up two gold medals. "This year, the medals are awarded to"—again the pause and smile—"Mrs. Florence Hockapuk and"—grin of teeth—"Mr. Eugenio Spritzer!"

Emil was furious.

After Florence and Eugenio went up to kiss the ring and claim their medals, Father Rogers had a final announcement.

"It is with deep sadness," he intoned, "that His Excellency accepts the resignation of Mr. Spritzer as Lay Director of the Life Saviors."

Bundeswehr caught Emil's eye. He didn't nod, and he didn't wink. I kept my word, he said with his black eyes.

Then came midnight Mass, celebrating the Savior reborn, a ritual joyous and lovely, the ceremonious panoply of which took Emil back across his years, back before his years, way back across all the centuries. He almost forgot about Spritzer, Nubs, duty, responsibility. Until Father Peter Creedmore came forward to give the sermon. He came in from the sacristy, where he had been waiting, not having entered earlier with all the other priests.

Waiting or hiding, Emil thought.

Emil had seen Father Creedmore in different situations, and each time the priest had exhibited a separate mood or pattern of behavior. Now, however, alone before a large audience, garbed in the vestments of priestly office and with no threat of being contradicted, Emil saw yet another Creedmore, wise, commanding, tolerant, anguished. It was as if Peter Creedmore, freed from the necessity of dealing with individual people, could transcend his own limitations and communicate with a thousand at once. He was candid.

"I know that many rumors have been bruited about in recent days."

He chose magnanimity.

"I want you all to know that I bear no malice toward any man."

Came down hard on the side of justice.

"The murderer *must* be caught, he *must* be caught and, God's will, he shall be caught!"

Cast a stone.

"I know that some men, eager but misguided, are prone to dash off hastily, not realizing the harm their false accusations cause."

Admitted his own failings.

"The Lord has given me a personality that is a cross to bear, a coat to wear, an old cloth coat of many tatters."

But thundered his deepest-held belief.

"It is not our call to judge our fellow man. Our Lord Jesus Christ shall be the judge, the only judge! BUT WE WORK HIS WILL UPON THIS EARTH."

Well, thought Emil.

Spritzer was not at the bishop's reception afterward, nor was Father Creedmore, nor were Ewald and Florence Hockapuk. Bundeswehr made sure that things went smoothly. Sarah received congratulations with happy restraint, Hugh talked with a lot of people he'd once known, most of whom wanted to know why he'd forsaken Stearns County for a place as far away as Iowa. Egg nog and Tom and Jerries were sipped, and, truth to tell, you could get a snort of schnapps if your taste ran along those lines.

Emil saw Dink and Ilsa Kufelski in the crush across the room, and walked over. Dink looked abashed but Ilsa was her usual self.

"Emil," she said, "I want you to know I just found out this afternoon what's been happening. I made Dink tell me." She turned to her husband. "Now, honey, you apologize to Emil for being such a chicken when he asked you to testify!"

"I apologize," Dink said, ducking his head.

"He'll do it any time you want!" Ilsa declared.

"Well, thanks, but things are pretty settled for the time being. Father Creedmore is off the hook, Eugenio's gone out of town. Corky says he's going to start a new investigation."

"Corky!" Ilsa laughed.

"Corky will be all right," Emil said. "Give him time."

"I just meant I don't think he'll do so hot on any investigation."

Emil didn't say so, but for a dark, private moment, he hoped she was right. If Nubs changed his mind and did not turn himself in, if Emil stayed silent . . .

The hour was late, and since the reception was more a formality than an actual party, the guests bade His Excellency good-bye.

"Well, Emil," exuded Bundeswehr, standing at the doorway, "cheer up and Merry Christmas. It's all over."

"Everybody seems to think so," Emil said.

23

A little after three, Christmas morning. Emil and Hugh were sitting in the living room, not saying much of anything, just being together. Last embers glowed and crackled in the fireplace. Hugh had his neck brace on again. He wasn't embarrassed about it anymore. Getting back from the bishop's mansion, he'd stumbled over something on the porch.

"What's this? It's a cane," he'd said.

"I—oh, I saw some kids playing with that earlier today," Emil replied hurriedly. "They must have left it here."

But Sarah wouldn't let him get away with it. "Don't let him hornswoggle you, Hugh," she'd said. "Emil had that knee thing again. I just hope it doesn't come back, with all the brandy he's been putting away!"

"Didn't you hear what Father Creedmore said?" Emil complained. "You're not supposed to judge your fellow man."

Sarah was ready for that. "It doesn't count with husbands."

Now Sarah and Dory were asleep, and the two old brothers were thinking about getting to bed themselves. But Emil was still worrying, and Hugh knew he was worrying, so they both sat there by the fire.

"Nubs on your mind, huh?" Hugh asked.

"Yes."

If I could just figure out what to do, Emil thought, then I'd be content. Should I talk to Nubs again? Do I file a report? Make the arrest? What?

Things known, unknown, suspected.

It was impossible to know who had gotten Trixie Miggs pregnant. Maybe she hadn't even known herself.

She was dead, though. That was for sure. So was her boy.

Emil remembered what Nubs had said over Tom and Jerries at his cabin: *I couldn't let Josh freeze to death under that tree after God had already decided that he should live.*

Emil shook his head.

"What is it?" asked Hugh.

"I was wrong about Father Creedmore. Guess I shouldn't have been so eager to judge."

"There's good counsel."

The fire burned low. Emil and Hugh sat watching it. A man can be comfortable with some people if they jabber away every minute. And he might be uncomfortable with a lot of people, no matter how easily the conversation flows. But simple silence is always fine. If Emil felt like saying something, he could. If Hugh felt like it, he would. And if neither did, it didn't matter.

The fire burned down. Emil got up from his rocking chair, felt a sudden twinge in his knee. He didn't want Hugh to notice, so he stretched elaborately. "Guess I'll hit the hay. See you in the mornin'."

"Figure it out about Nubs?"

"Yes. I'm goin' to buy him a new dog and take it out to his place tomorrow. You can come along."

Emil crossed the living room and started upstairs, trying not to limp.

"Good-night, Emil," Hugh said. "And go easy on that leg. It's taken us one hell of a way."

"Guess so," said Emil. "But, as Father Creedmore told us tonight, we work His will on this earth. Sometimes it slows a man down."

For everything there is a season,
and a time for every purpose
under heaven:
> *a time to be born, and a time to die;*
> *a time to sow, and a time to reap;*
> *a time to kill . . .*

—Ecclesiastes